A Breath Away

The Final Chapter Of Life

J. JUDSON LACKO

A BREATH AWAY

This book is written to provide information and motivation to readers. Its purpose is not to render any type of psychological, legal, or professional advice of any kind. The content is the sole opinion and expression of the author, and not necessarily that of the publisher.

Printed in the United States of America.

ISBN 978-1-949746-93-8 (Paperback)
ISBN 978-1-949746-94-5 (Digital)

Lettra Press books may be ordered through booksellers or by contacting:

Lettra Press LLC
18229 E 52nd Ave.
Denver City, CO 80249
1 303 586 1431 | info@lettrapress.com
www.lettrapress.com

Contents

Contents

Chapter 1

A Look Back to the Beginning

The new fallen autumn leaves danced in a circle on the pavement as Chris made the right turn onto the driveway to the front of the house as he had done so many times before, fifty years ago. He had lived over half of a century since high school graduation, his life was coming to its finality, and the awareness of his own mortality was being realized. He cherished his time left.

The garage door slowly rose as Chris got out of the car, and Elise's daughter walked toward him as he closed the car door.

She smiled and extended her hand. As Chris looked at her, he could see Elise's face looking back at him.

"Hi. I'm Cassy," She said as their extended hands met. She sounded like her mother. If Chris had closed his eyes, he could have sworn he was seventeen years old again.

"Hi, Cassy, I'm Chris Logan. I dated your mother our senior year in high school."

As they walked into the garage, into the basement and headed up the stairs to the kitchen, memories rushed back of those times Elise and Chris spent together in the family room, playing records and dancing. They could only see each other once a week because they lived in different school districts, twelve miles apart.

Chapter 2

A Past Remembrance

As Cassy and Chris ascended the steps to the kitchen, Chris remembered one Friday night in the winter of 1961. Elise hadn't heard his car drive up the driveway and was sitting on the couch in the basement family room, looking through pictures in a photo album. The window in the basement facing the couch was frosted over, but Chris could see into the basement from the landing, as the snow swirled around the window glass. It was next to the steps that led to the front door. He bent down and looked through the window and watched the girl who held his heart in the secret recesses of her heart as she turned the pages of the album, casually smiling as she looked over the photographs. Her dark auburn hair was full and flowing. Her bangs just slightly covered the top of her glasses, her dark brown eyes were lost in the pages before her. She was wearing his favorite light blue angora pull-over sweater with a large 'cowl collar', and dark blue pants. Her feet were tucked under her like a fashion model, her hands rested on her lap as she paused for each page of photographs. Chris stood there watching her for several moments. Watching her, not wanting to end the moment, his mind began to explore the feelings that drifted into the night like snowflakes:

Winter's Rhapsody

Moonbeams scampering to and fro,
Running wild, across the snow,
Scampering free in pure delight
In the cold and wintery night.

Shadows fall – and cast a spell,
On places old I know so well –
As on I walk across this sea
Of snow - In Winter's Rhapsody!

Mem'ries sweet – And mem'ries sad
Things that made our young hearts glad,
All of these return to me,
As on I move across this sea.

Wondering on – midst falling snow –
In the moonbeams gentle glow,
Gives me time to reminisce
Upon this time of happiness.

Little walks on nights like this,
A warm caress – A gentle kiss.
Love in bloom for all to see –
Completed – Winter's Rhapsody!

Ah, - But mem'ries fade from sight
Off into the wintery night,
As to my Love my footsteps go,
Pressing down the soft white snow.

Moonbeams still come break the night,
And scamper free – in pure delight!
And our love meets in purity,
This is our Winter's Rhapsody!

This was the first poem Chris had written for Elise. He chose to save it for a special occasion.

Finally, he climbed the steps to the front door and knocked. Her mother opened the door and let him in.

"How long were you going to stand out there in the snow, Chris?" she asked.

"I'm sorry, Mrs. Hunter. I was enjoying the snow."

By this time, Elise had come up from the basement. She walked over to Chris, smiling.

"Miss me?" She asked, "I was beginning to think you weren't coming over. I was just going through some old family albums. Would you like to join me downstairs?"

Elise wasn't allowed to date until her eighteenth birthday, so they could never go anywhere, but Chris could see her at her home.

She placed her head on his shoulder as they descended the stairs to the basement. As soon as their feet touched the floor, they embraced each other as they always did, softly at first, then held each other as if neither of them would ever let go. Their lips would slowly meet in a long passionate kiss. They gazed into each other's eyes, flowing gently back and forth into each other's souls, savoring the time shared with each other within.

"I love you, Elise," Chris whispered. "I've missed you."

"I love you, Chris," She spoke softly, nestling her head against his chest. "I miss you from the time you leave me to go home, until you come back to me."

The first kiss they shared when they held each other was always one that melted away the time that seemed to linger between them when they were apart.

Chris put a stack of records on the 45 rpm record player, as their evening together opened into the fantasy which was theirs alone. Just as quickly as their time together began, it ended. Chris had to leave, too wait another week to be with her.

Chapter 3
How They Met

Cassy and Chris reached the top of the stairs, went through the kitchen, and into the living room. There was a couch with its back to the bay window in the living room. Two over-stuffed chairs with an end table between them faced the couch.

Cassy asked Chris to sit on the couch, and she sat across from him.

"From what you indicated in your email, you were wondering what Mom did after she started nurse's training." Cassy began as she settled into the chair.

Cassy and Chris sat talking about Elise for well over an hour. Cassy went over her mother's life from the time Chris and Elise separated. Elise continued her sophomore year at Bartlett Hospital School of Nursing, and started dating a former classmate from high school, Bill Potter. They were married at the end of her senior year in training, she became pregnant with Cassy within the year.

Chris told her about Taylor Wagner, the reason for his breakup with Elise, his own lack of maturity which caused them to part from his first experience with college life, his leaving college due to a poor Q.P.A. (0.9), four years in the United States Air Force, finally getting a degree and certification in Medical Technology, and the years that followed, entering the field of Emergency Medical Services and teaching in two different universities and three technical trade schools.

"I've wondered why you two stopped seeing each other. Mom told me you would always hold a special place in her heart, even though she loved Dad. You two seemed to have something that few find. I never told her, but I sensed you had sort of a 'soul mate' relationship."

Chris didn't know that Elise had discussed their relationship with Cassy in such detail, though it didn't surprise him. He felt a little uncomfortable not knowing to what extent she had shared the details of their relationship. Chris looked over at Cassy, and started to explain how they had met.

"A friend of mine and I were looking for something to do one Saturday night. It was in June, right before my senior year. we found out about teenage dances the YMCA held in West Centerville, so that's where we went."

"I remember walking down the steps to the lower floor at the YMCA, stepping onto the floor, I looked over to my right where the girls were standing, waiting to dance. It's odd, but as I looked down the row, my eyes met your mother's eyes and stayed transfixed. I stopped. I told my friend I'd see him later, walking over to your mother. Our eyes had not lost contact. I held out my hand, taking her hand in mine, asking her to dance. She hesitated for a moment, then walked onto the dance floor with me".

As they danced, they introduced themselves to each other, talking about things high school teens talk about. The dance ended all too soon. Chris made his way across the room to where his friend was standing.

"Well, John, did you dance with anyone yet?"

"Naw," he replied, "how about you?"

Chris smiled, "Yeah. I did. Her name is Elise. She goes to West Central High School and lives about a mile from here. She's in the band, plays clarinet and wants to become a nurse."

John looked somewhat surprised.

"One dance, and you got all that? A little fast, don't you think?" John asked, scanning the room for a possible dance partner.

"What do YOU think?" Chris replied looking over where Elise was sitting, turned heading back in her direction. Chris danced every dance with her that night. He asked her if he could take her home, but she said her father was taking her and her girlfriend Mary Lynne home after the dance. Chris told her he was glad to have met her and said he hoped to see her the following week. She said she would be there, and was glad she had met him.

The next week dragged by. He hadn't asked her for her phone number, so he was kind of in limbo.

The following Saturday night finally came. Chris went back to the YMCA. He walked in, descended the steps to the recreation room, looking towards the place Elise had been the previous Saturday. He didn't see her. He began looking around the room. She was dancing with someone else, but once again, when their eyes met, they smiled at each other, and Chris knew he was going to spend another evening with her.

The dance finished, and Elise walked over to Chris, smiling.

"Miss me?" she asked, as their hands joined together.

"I'll always miss you," Chris said as he put his arm around her waist.

The next dance was another slow dance ('Earth Angel'). They made their way through the people standing around the floor. At last they were in each other's arms, slowing moving across the floor. Elise pulled Chris close to her, laying her head on his shoulder.

"Can I tell you something, Chris?" she said softly. "I was afraid you might not come back. I enjoyed last Saturday so much. Mary Lynne wanted to know why I was so happy. I know this sounds silly, but I felt so good when we were together. I couldn't wait for tonight to come and see you."

Chris couldn't believe what he was hearing!

He pulled back a little, looking deeply into her eyes.

"Keep those feelings, Elise. I feel the same way. I couldn't wait to be with you again."

They danced every slow dance that night. As the night ended, Chris asked Elise again if he could take her home.

"My parents won't allow me to date until I'm eighteen. I can meet you here, but my dad insists he take me home. I'm sorry."

Elise started to look down toward the floor. Chris cupped his hand under her chin, lifting her head until their eyes met.

"That's okay. We have at least four hours a week we can still share, being together."

She pulled him closer to her as they danced, and nestled her head on his shoulder. Apparently, they were dancing a little too close, because one of the chaperons came over and tapped Chris on the shoulder.

"Son, if you dance any closer to the young lady, you'll be behind her."

Chris apologized. Elise and Chris 'readjusted' their distance between each other. They slipped back into their own world as the music played, the other couples faded into the night. Elise and Chris's moments together raced away. Finally, the last dance of the night was announced.

As the last strains of the last dance ended, Elise and Chris held each other tenderly for the last time for another week. This time he was not going to let her go without her phone number.

"Elise ... Do you think I could have your phone number?" Chris managed to ask.

She pulled a piece of paper from her pocket, and handed it to him.

"Do you honestly think I was going to let you walk away without it?" she said, as she placed the paper in his hand.

Their relationship had now begun and was to continue.

Chapter 4
No More Doubt

Elise and Chris continued seeing each other throughout their senior year and talked about their future. Chris was planning on becoming a physician and Elise was going to nurse's training at Bartlett Memorial Hospital. Chris's Pre-med studies were to be at Craig/Sanderson College and medical school would be completed at the University of Pittsburgh, if possible.

By the time the summer had faded into colorful autumn, they knew that this relationship was destined too last. There was one incident, however, that almost ended it. Chris arrived at Elise's home around 7:30 on a Saturday evening, and her best friend, Mary Lynne, met him at the bottom of the front steps.

She had a rather silly grin on her face.

"Elise is back on the patio," she said.

They proceeded toward the back of the house, and for some reason, Chris began feeling a little uncomfortable. Elise was sitting under the grape arbor on the left side of the patio. She was wearing a white blouse with a sweater over it due to an evening chill, and a dark skirt. As usual, she was wearing a pair of flats. (Chris couldn't remember a time she didn't wear flats.)

As he walked over to her, she rose from the chair, but she kept her head down. Finally, she did look up into his eyes.

"Hi. How was your week?" she asked.

"Fine, and yours?" Chris answered.

He sat down on the lawn chair across from her. '*What is going on*?' He thought to himself.

Elise and Mary Lynne kept looking at each other as they talked about trivial things. Elise started playing with something that was suspended on a chain around her neck. Chris realized that there was a class ring at the end of the chain! The ring wasn't his! His stomach started twisting in knots. He didn't know what to say. He didn't know what to do. His hearing began to shut down. Elise and Mary Lynne were talking, but it was gibberish in his brain. He sat there trying to smile and look as if he hadn't noticed the ring.

Chris did the only thing he felt he could do. He stood up, and began to walk away as calmly as possible.

"I think I better go.", he said, turning and starting down the walk toward the front of the house.

Mary Lynne followed quickly behind him.

"Wait! Wait! Chris! Don't leave."

"You better give Bill's ring back to me, Elise," Mary Lynne said, "or Chris is going to leave, and not come back."

Chris couldn't believe it. Elise was testing him to see if he was jealous!

He loved Elise and couldn't consider her being with someone else.

He didn't know if he should be angry or grateful that she wasn't seeing someone else.

Chris stopped, turned and looked at Elise, and then looked at Mary Lynne.

Elise removed the chain from her neck and handed it to Mary Lynne.

"I think Elise and I have to talk."

Mary Lynne knew what Chris meant, and hurried down the walk to her car.

Elise walked over to Chris, head tilted down, trembling, her heart aching, not knowing what he was going to do or say. She realized how deeply she had hurt him.

It was all Chris could do to speak. He felt crushed inside, but he didn't want to lose her.

"Elise, why would you do this? We write to each other every day. We spend hours on the phone every week. I've accepted the fact that you and I can't go out on dates in the car until you're eighteen years old. What more do you want me to do to show you what you mean to me?

Then the final reason came from Chris's lips, without his realizing it.

"I love you, Elise," Chris said, as he took her in his arms. "I want us to enjoy the beauty in our lives. I want us to cherish the smell of rain as it refreshes our times together. I want us to feel the touch of a breeze upon our faces. I want us to fight together to fulfill our dreams. I want us to plan our lives together. Most of all, I want you to love me as I love you. I want you to continue to make my life what it is. I want it to continue to make me what I am."

Elise stared toward the ground the whole time Chris was talking, afraid to see what was in his eyes, afraid to see disappointment and the hurt she had caused him.

She raised her head slowly and their eyes met.

"I've never had anyone …" Elise said hesitating, "love me," giving way to the hurt she felt in her heart.

She placed her warm hands on his arms.

"Please forgive me, Chris. I know you love me, and I love you. I wouldn't blame you if you wanted to walk away, and never look back. I'm asking you not too. I'm asking you to forgive me, and stay, … Please,… I believe we belong together."

Chris embraced her and held her so close they could feel the warmth of their bodies next to each other. He kissed her, slowly, deliberately. He could feel the tears from her cheek on his face. They both understood their love was now secure.

Once more their eyes met, and all doubt disappeared. Any doubt either of them had, had slipped away into the abbess of extinction.

They walked back up the walkway to the patio to the swing under the arbor. They sat down on the swing and slowly moved close together.

Chris, now secure in his love for Elise, opened his heart to her as he had never done before.

"Elise, this may not be the right time, perhaps not even the right place. What I'm trying so hard to say, is that I want you. I'm asking you to be my wife, to never leave me, to plan our lives and futures as one, together. I know you'll probably think this is silly, but I was at the mall today and found these in a little shop. I know they're just costume jewelry, but I bought them to have you try them on, to see how they would look on your finger."

Chris reached into his pocket, pulling out an engagement ring and a wedding ring.

"I know we're eighteen, and we both have a long way to go in our education, but I want to know that marriage is in our future. Is it in the future, Elise? Will you marry me?"

Elise's reaction was immediate. She was smiling, and couldn't believe what she was hearing. She put her arms around Chris hugging him. She placed his head between her hands, gazed into his eyes, her eyes sparkling, and said, "Yes, Chris, yes, Of course, I'll marry you," kissing him ever so gently at first, then more passionately as they shared this special moment.

"I love you, Chris. You complete my life. You will always be with me, no matter where I am."

Chris slowly placed the rings on the third finger of her left hand. She moved her hand out into the light, sighing.

"I wish I could wear the engagement ring now", she sighed," This all seems so right between us. I want to tell the world how much we love each other".

They stood there for a while, locked in an embrace, saying so much, speaking only with their eyes.

Chris watched Elise remove the rings from her hand and slip them into her pocket, wishing they could stay on her finger, but no-one else could see them for a while. Nothing ever felt so good to Chris before. Here they were with at least four years of education for her, and eight years of education for him before they could be man and wife, yet together, their future had been set in motion. Now came the hard part. The long days between seeing each other, the nights they could only look toward the sky, dreaming of the day they would be forever together, knowing love would hold them together always.

Chapter 5

Off to College

Nurse's training began in August of 1962. Elise had to spend six weeks at Seaton Hill College campus in Latrobe, Pennsylvania, to be trained in certain required college courses before she could begin her floor work back at Bartlett Memorial Hospital. Chris went to Seaton Hill to visit her in the last week of August. It was like an "Open House" visit for relatives and friends of the student nurses.

The campus was beautiful. The stately buildings, the towering trees, walkways everywhere. Flowers of all sorts in little gardens and lining the walkways.

As Chris headed for the dormitory, Elise was in her room putting the final touches on her make-up. Her roommate, Megan, was lying across her bed reading a book.

"So, tell me, Elise, how did you and Chris meet?" Megan asked, turning the page in her book, "What was the attraction?"

Elise looked at Megan, and pondered for a moment before answering the question.

"We met at a YMCA dance. My friend, Mary Lynne, and I would go there on Saturday nights. It gave us a chance to meet guys, and dance and have a good time, since I wasn't allowed to date until I was eighteen, it was the only way I could get out of the house and socialize. The night that we met was somehow different. For some reason, when I walked down the stairs to the recreation room, I looked around, as if I was expecting see someone I had not seen in a long time. It was almost as if I were in a trance.

"How's that?", Megan asked.

Elise stared into space for a moment, and then answered.

"I felt like something was going to happen that night, something wonderful," Elise continued, "I can't explain it, but when Chris walked down the steps to the recreation room and stopped, turning his head towards me, our eyes met, sending a wave of self-awareness and calm over me, something I had never experienced before. The feeling came from my heart and I wanted him to come over and ask me to dance. My eyes saw him and I couldn't look away. He just stood there for a minute, looking back at me, then slowly walked over, took me by the hand, and asked me to dance. He was about six feet tall… sandy hair … dark brown eyes, and a smile that stays with you."

Megan looked up from her book.

"It sounds to me like the beginning of a 'Cinderella' story …" Megan said.

Elise looked at herself in her mirror.

"It was,", Elise sighed, "Somehow I knew it was a new beginning in my life. I felt Chris was going to be a part of my life for a long time to come."

"Anything else about him you liked?", Megan asked.

Elise thought for a moment.

"Yes," she said, smiling, "The way he treated me. Very polite, very gentle, and a good conversationalist, even though he seemed a little nervous at first. His voice was soft and pleasant. The way he held me as we danced. I could feel the warmth from his touch on my waist and how it showed a certain caring. I don't know, it was almost surreal. I didn't want to dance or be held by anyone but him. He apparently felt the same way, because we danced the whole night together. At the end of the evening, we were talking and laughing like we had known each other for years."

"So, did you tell him you loved him that night?", Megan said sarcastically.

Elise just looked down at Megan.

Hesitating slightly, she replied. "...No... as a matter of fact, he told me he loved me first. That didn't happen for another four weeks. Oh, by the way... he asked me to marry him. You know, I said 'yes' without thinking or hesitation!"

"See you later, Megan", Elise said as she hurried out the door and down the steps to meet Chris.

Chris went to Elise's dormitory, and stopped at the desk to call to her room. While he was dialing the phone, Chris saw her coming down the stairway, smiling as she always did when they met after being separated for a while.

They embraced, and kissed.

"Hi, Angel. You don't know how happy I am to see you," Chris said as they joined hands.

"Miss me?" She asked.

"Just a little," Chris responded, "As a matter of fact, I wrote something for you."

He reached into his pocket and took out a poem he had written.

"I hope you like it. I wrote it to show you how I feel about us, Angel."

She looked down at the poem.

"Chris," she said smiling, "You're so thoughtful. Thank you."

They walked over to a bench shaded by an overhanging tree and sat down.

Elise recited the words from the poem:

ONE

You are me – and I am You – and all that we are, we are together.
There is not a day without a sunrise – nor is there a day that begins
Without thoughts of you.

You are me – and I am you – and all that we are, we are together.
Whether locked within strife - or locked within a warm embrace -
We share those moments – knowing what we feel within –
And thus our love survives.

You are me – and I am you – and all that we are, we are together.
Be it a thousand miles distant – you are just a thought away –
And your essence swells within, and warms me to the depth of
My soul.

You are me – and I am you – and all that we are, we are together.
We will love – We will share – We will grow – together.

She finished reading, set the poem in her lap, and looked up at him.

"Chris, It's beautiful. You're right: 'All we are, we are together'."

Chris put his arm around Elise and pulled her close, kissing her.

"I'll never be able to tell you in a lifetime, how much you mean to me. You are my heart. You are my love. You are my 'breath away.'"

Chapter 6

Separation

Elise's father finally permitted them to car-date after her eighteenth birthday in May. Chris appreciated her a lot more, after waiting so long.

Summer came and went so quickly that year. Elise and Chris had to get use to her schedule at Seaton Hill, and her floor assignments at the hospital.

Finally, the first week in September, Chris started his freshman semester at Craig/Sanderson College. Chris had never been away from home for an extended period before, and that started the undoing of the firm relationship he had with Elise. She was so much more mature than Chris, like eighteen going on thirty-five. She was focused and knew what she wanted in life. She had become a woman overnight, and Chris was way behind in how to deal with life; that life didn't revolve around him and what it meant to be faithful.

Chris had to work for his room and board at the college in the college cafeteria. It was there that he met Taylor Wagner, a freshman from New York City. They both were lonely, not knowing anyone on campus, and seemed to be drawn to each other. They just started talking one day and one thing led to another, and the next thing Chris knew, they were seeing each other every day and dating.

Taylor stood about five-foot seven, had long light brown hair, sky blue eyes, and a near perfect torso. Her voice was slightly high pitched, but beautiful to listen to. She was a little pigeon toed, but that didn't detract from her natural beauty.

Taylor always seemed to know what to say, as Chris discovered later. She could easily manipulate people.

They worked in the cafeteria together. She had the early shift of noon to four o'clock in the afternoon, and Chris worked the three o'clock shift until seven o'clock.

They would usually meet after Chris's shift ended at Statler Hall girl's dormitory, and just walked around the campus, or sit on a bench in front of the fountain in the park, in front of the Administration Building.

They would hold hands, and as night would settle on the campus, they would hold each other.

There was a ritual that they, as freshman, had to participate in, which was the 'painting of the rocks' which spelled out 'Craig/ Sanderson College' at the top of the hill, by the reservoir leading into the small town of South Wayne. So, on a Friday afternoon, the Freshman Class, wearing old clothes and shoes, hiked up to the reservoir with their advisors, and painted the rocks with white wash. They got white wash over the rocks, and over them! But they had a good time, laughing and carrying on.

The class descended the hill back to the college an hour later, walking down the hill, walking where they wanted. Taylor and Chris took the long way back, past the church leading into town, on over to the first park of five parks. the one that had the Bridge of the Two Pines. In winter, if it was snowing, couples would go under the huge pines and make out at night, until the local police patrol would shine their spotlight into the trees, and catch them in, shall we say, compromising positions!... The police would simply tell them to 'take it elsewhere', and move on. No-one was ever arrested.

They walked on to the bridge, and stopped by the railing in the middle of the bridge (the bridge was only about fourteen feet long).

Chris leaned up against the iron railing, and Taylor faced him, their bodies meeting, their arms encompassed each other, and for the first time, Chris kissed her. Her response was more than Chris had expected, and they held the kiss for almost a minute.

Chris pulled away from her slowly, and looked in to her eyes.

"Taylor, where did THAT come from?", he asked, trying to get his blood pressure down, regain his composure, and stop shaking!

Taylor just continued to look longingly into his eyes.

"I've wanted to do that for some time, Chris", Taylor replied, "I hope you feel the same way."

Chris was feeling just the opposite. He was feeling the first pangs of guilt. He hadn't kissed another girl since he began dating Elise. What was he thinking?! This wasn't right. Chris had crossed the line. He had betrayed Elise's love.

They kissed once more, and the passion of the kiss was deeper than the first kiss. Chris gave way to natural instincts and pulled Taylor close to him, and she moaned softly and increased the intensity of her embrace. Chris's head was spinning, and feelings that he had shared only with Elise were, in some ways, surfacing with Taylor.

"I…I think we better slow down, Taylor. We need to think about what's going on here," Chris said, pulling away from her.

"I don't have to think, Chris. I know what I feel." Taylor answered, pressing herself closer to him.

Chris pulled away once more.

"I'm walking you back to the dorm, Taylor. This is a little overwhelming for me. This shouldn't be happening."

Taylor hesitated, but she knew that he would need the time to understand what was happening between them.

They walked back to her dorm in silence, holding each other's hands.

They walked up the steps to the front door, stopped, and she drew Chris close to her and kissed him.

"This is us, Chris," Taylor whispered in his ear as they embraced. "Don't let it go. I think I'm falling in love with you."

"I need some time, Taylor, to think about this. I'll call you later tonight.", Chris replied as he slowly released her from his arms, turned, and walked back down the stairs, returning to his dorm. This situation was not going to be easy to resolve. Why had he broken his trust with Elise? Chris had never been in a relationship before that made him feel guilt.

Chris continued to write to Elise, but the letters slowly began to get shorter and shorter. He had to stay on campus for the first four weeks, so he couldn't get home to see Elise to clear his conscious. He knew he had developed deep feelings for Taylor, and was confused as to what to do. Maturity remained foreign to him.

College Homecoming was coming up in November, and Chris had planned to take Elise, but he knew her father probably wouldn't let her come.

He planned to go home and try and convince her father to let her come to South Wayne for the Homecoming festivities.

Taylor had expected to go to Homecoming with Chris, since they were seeing so much of each other, in her mind, they were now a couple. She didn't take the news well when Chris told her he had already asked Elise.

"Why would you take her?" Taylor asked indignantly, when Chris told her his intentions.

"We're together now. By November, she won't be a part of your life anymore. You'll be with me."

Chris didn't exactly share that view. For the first time in his life, Chris was torn between the love of two woman. Taylor was here and now. Elise was sixty miles away from him, and he couldn't see her or be with her, like he was with Taylor. He really didn't know what to do about this situation, but he knew he had to decide soon.

Taylor was aware of Elise, but Elise knew nothing about Taylor, or so it seemed. Decision time came on Chris's fifth week at college, as he headed home to see Elise.

Chris called her when he arrived home and Elise she had no duty scheduled on her floor for the weekend. He asked her if he could see her that night.

There was a slight pause in her speech.

"I guess so, Chris. What's wrong?"

Chris thought Elise knew, but she didn't seem to show it.

"I just need to talk to you about the Homecoming dance," Chris managed to stumble through.

Once again, Elise paused.

"I'll see you about seven o'clock then. Do you want me to just dress casual?" She asked.

Chris noticed a change in her voice tone.

"Never mind. I'll just pick something out. I'll see you tonight. I love you.", then she hung up the phone.

Chris drove onto her driveway at exactly seven o'clock, and Elise was waiting at the top of the steps that led down to the driveway. He didn't have time to get out of the car once he had stopped. She hurried down the steps and got into the car before Chris could even say "Hello."

She stayed on the far side of the seat, and made no attempt to move over next to him.

"Now," she began in a very controlled tone of voice, (Chris had never experienced this side of her) "What's going on with the Homecoming Dance? I explained to you that my father won't allow me to travel that far. I would have to stay overnight. You know my dad. That just isn't going to happen."

Chris was some-what dumbfounded by her head-on approach. It was like talking to a different person.

"Now look, Elise, I put up with not being able to take you out or pick you up all last year. You're in nurse's training and you should be able to have a little more breathing room as far as our dating goes."

Elise just looked at Chris and folded her arms, which in body language, says 'keep talking but you're talking to the hand!'

Chris complained to her the twelve-mile drive back to his home without her responding. He pulled in the driveway in front of his house, and stopped the car.

There was a moment of silence between them as Elise faced Chris.

"Are you done?" Elise asked softly, a tear dropping from her eye, tilting her head, not to the 'Miss me?' side, but to the side where she controlled the situation at hand.

She was just staring at Chris, her arms folded in front of her.

Then, in a low controlled tone, she spoke.

"Who is she, Chris, and how long have you been seeing her?"

Chris could see his betrayal in Elise's face, the hurt that engulfed her heart.

What could he say? She had just shot him down. Chris had crashed and was burning. She knew from the time she got into the car until now that there was someone else in his life. In some respects, she had known all along.

"Her name's Taylor. She's a freshman from New York City. We've worked together in the cafeteria for the past month."

Chris looked down toward the floor, as he tried to figure out how he would explain. For this situation, however, there could be no explanation – no defense - It was a betrayal. There was dead silence for about a minute, and Chris looked up toward Elise's face. The smile he had been used to which filled him with love and happiness had been replaced with a disappointed frown. Her dark eyes that would look in to his and shared their souls together were now vacant and disbelieving. Her heart bled out the trust they shared together. Chris's love for her had turned into a lie.

Chris hesitated. "I don't know what to say, Angel," Chris began, "Taylor and I…"

"Please don't call me 'Angel' while you're talking to me about … (She twitched her one nostril in derision)… Taylor." Elise broke in, in a cold tone. She was holding back her emotions, and her self-control was firm.

"It just seemed to happen," Chris continued, "She and I both needed someone to care for, to talk to, to listen to, and to share our emotions from time to time. I guess what it came down to was she was there, and I lost my self-control. I wanted to be a part of the college life and have someone there to share it with."

With that explanation, the knife of betrayal had buried itself deep into Elise's trusting heart.

Her jaw began to tighten up. Chris had had no idea how she would take this.

"Is this it then, Chris? You're just ending everything that we've shared together and taking what would have been our future and letting it go? Don't you think I knew how you felt about our dating situation? You, wanting to be with me, knowing how you put up with Dad's restrictions just so we had SOME time we could share together, alone? What of the night you ask me to marry you, and asked me to never leave you? Do I stop loving you? Stop caring? What about our future? Has that been tossed aside, too? Is this what you're asking me to do, Chris? Were those just words you said that night? Were those words only for the moment, or were they vows you gave to me, never to lose their meaning? I'll be here for you always. I need to know you'll be here for me. I wish I could have stopped this from happening. I can only tell you what's in my heart. This storm that's passing between us. This isn't in our plans, Chris, this can't be our future."

Chris had been looking in to her eyes the whole time. Perhaps for the first time in his life, stopped thinking about himself, and was seeing the person next to him as the one who loved him and wanted to share her life with.

She moved closer to Chris, and wrapped her arms around him. Tears filled her eyes.

She said something to Chris, which came as a complete surprise.

"I'm not going to let this happen, Chris. I love you too much to let you go. You're going to go back to school and tell this Taylor person that you won't be seeing her anymore. It's over between the two of you. Remember the poem you wrote to me about how 'I am you and you are me? What we are, we are together'. If what you wrote is true, then she has no place in a relationship with you. Tell me, Chris, is what you wrote the truth? or was it a lie?"

Chris couldn't believe it! Elise was FORGIVING him, FIGHTING for him, even though he had betrayed her love.

Each reached out for the other and they held each other for a long period of time. Gradually, they faced each other and joined their lips in a kiss that started softly, and ended in the passion that was theirs alone. Finally, Chris drew back and looked deep into her eyes.

"You're right, Elise. You are me and I am you, what we are, we are together."

It was still early and Chris didn't want to drive Elise home yet, so they went for a drive to the Greater Pittsburgh Airport, as they did from time to time, and walked up to the observation deck to watch the planes as they taxied to and from the terminal, and then went to the take-off positions. They loved standing on the observation deck, with the wind swirling around them from the ramp. They would talk about how someday it would be them on one of those jets, traveling to places in their dreams. They held hands, and she would lay her head on Chris's shoulder, look up at him, and once again would share a kiss. It was truly a night to remember for them.

Chapter 7

Return to Taylor

Chris returned to the college campus that Sunday morning and met Taylor on the Bridge of the Two Pines, in the park across from the church. Chris was standing on the bridge as she walked across the grass. She seemed slightly nervous as she approached him.

"Well, how did Elise take the news about us?" she asked, trying to show some hope with a slight smile.

"Taylor, I didn't end it with Elise. When I was with her, it was like we had never been separated from each other. I'm still in love with her, and that isn't going to change."

Taylor stopped where she was and stared at Chris in disbelief.

"What about us? What about all we shared this past month? How I took care of you when you were so sick with the flu, our plans to be together. Doesn't that count for anything? and our times alone together, sharing our feelings, OUR love. What about that? Or did you just say those things to be with me? Tell me, Chris. What's to happen to me now?"

She walked to the rail on the side of the bridge, her head down, her eyes awash with tears. Chris eased over towards her, and stood behind her.

"What we shared, we shared. I was lonely, and you were lonely. We both needed the affection to keep ourselves uplifted and able to cope with being away from home, each of us supporting the other."

"I felt some guilt at the times we were together, but when I was with Elise, the guilt I felt was soul wrenching. I had betrayed her love. I couldn't go on living a lie."

Taylor turned around and looked in Chris's eyes. Her blue eyes were pools of tears. She drew close to him, put her arms around him and kissed him, like she had never done before. His head was spinning. She stopped crying after a while, and calmed down, wiping the tears from her face.

"Alright," she asked, "Where do WE go from here?"

Chris wasn't sure what to say. He knew what the answer should be, but he failed to commit to it.

She continued.

"Would you mind doing me a favor? Walk with me for a while. I need to be right with your decision. I don't feel like being alone right now.

"Sure", Chris said. "Where would you like to go?"

"Just walk with me… Where we go… We go…" she replied.

They walked through each of the parks in front of the college, and as they walked, Taylor would point out the different experiences associated with the park and their relationship.

The first park going towards the college was where they came after they painted the rocks up at the reservoir. She remembered them laughing and holding hands, and on one of their walks together, going to the gazebo at the end of the park, where they shared a kiss.

The next park, they took the path to the center, where there was a fountain with the water spraying in the middle. There were benches around the fountain. Taylor remembered they would sit in the afternoon after classes and before they had to go to work in the cafeteria. They spent many sessions there getting to know each other.

The last park they walked through was Monument Park. At the beginning of the park is a monument to those who served in the Civil

War. Most would never take notice looking at it, but it faced south, and according to local rumors, it was faced in that direction to show where the county's sympathies lay, as far as the war was concerned.

They walked down to a little diner opposite the science hall. It looked like the type you would see in the old movies. They had eaten there many times at lunch and between classes. They went inside, sat in a booth, and ordered some lunch.

As they ate, Taylor continued to talk about all the places and things they had shared.

After they finished eating, they walked back up the hill, walked between the Administration building and the Business building, and up to Statler Hall, which was her dormitory.

They ascended the steps, and stopped outside the front door.

"Thank you for taking the time to walk with me." she said.

Taylor looked up into Chris's eyes once more and kissed him long and hard, while pressing her body to his.

"I don't want this to end, Chris. I don't want to be without you."

She was crying, and pressed her face into his shoulder.

"Please, please, stay with me. This doesn't have to end. I love you. I love you so much." They just stood there, looking into each other's eyes.

Taylor had very skillfully worked her way back into his life by taking that walk with him. Chris was drawn right into what she was saying.

"Taylor," Chris began, "I need some time to sort this all out, to make it clear in my own mind. I know I must choose between you and Elise, but right now, I can't make a sound decision."

She looked back into his eyes and pulled him close again.

"Whatever you decide, I'll accept."

Chris then turned away and proceeded down the steps to the walk that lead to his dormitory.

Chapter 8
The Letters

Chris returned to his room in Hammond House, the dormitory where he resided. He went up to his room and sat at his study desk trying to figure out what to do. Finally, he decided it was unfair for Elise not to have the opportunity to date as he had done and see if their love was as real as they thought it was. He still was unable to recognize his own lack of maturity. He missed the entire question. He was placing the whole dilemma on Elise rather than himself. To justify it, he was going to have her do what he had done.

Chris composed a letter to send to Elise at Seaton Hill.

He wrote: 'Dear Elise, I did as you requested and saw Taylor to tell her that it was over between her and I. She pointed out the many things we had shared together, and took a long walk to talk about our relationship. By the time we got back to her dormitory, I wasn't sure what my feelings were. I only know no matter which of you I am with, I will have hurt the other more than I know or can understand.

I feel that we should separate for the time being in order that I might find where my true feelings lay. Perhaps you should date also. I never meant to hurt you. If nothing else, please believe that.

Chris's lack of maturity was putting the separation on Elise, who had maintained her loyalty, and was guilty of nothing but loving him.

Please return my ring. Love, Chris.

Chapter 9

Elise Receives the Letter

Elise had just finished her 10 o'clock biology class, and since she didn't have another class until 2 o'clock, went back to the dormitory, stopped at the mail room, picked up Chris's letter, and headed for her room to read it.

Megan Stern, her roommate was sitting on her bed, doing her nails, when Elise walked in.

"Letter from Chris, Elise?" she asked.

"Yes," She answered, smiling, walking around Megan's bed to her side of the room. Elise had hardly read through the first lines of the letter, when she threw the letter on the bed, pulled Chris's ring off her finger, and threw it to the other side of the room.

Tears streamed down her face as she walked over, picked up the ring, and threw it back to the other side of the room.

"I… I don't believe it! How can he just stop loving me, just like that!"

Megan jumped up from her bed and grabbed Elise.

"Elise! Elise! Calm down! Throwing that ring around the room won't help!"

Elise turned, and put her arms around Megan, sobbing, as her heart broke and waves of disbelief flowed from the wound.

"Megan, what am I going to do? I just can't stop what I feel."

Elise pulled away from Megan, went over to her nightstand, and pushed everything that was on it to the floor, went to her dresser and threw everything off the dresser to the floor. Still sobbing, face bright red, she went to her bed, tore all the covers off the bed on to the floor. After reading the first lines of the letter, Elise's mind had begun to spin. The betrayal was ripping her heart apart. There was nothing she could do.

Elise placed her hands over her eyes and collapsed on top of the bed coverings, and cried herself to sleep.

Megan sat on the side of Elise's bed, stroking Elise's hair as her friend drifted off. Megan softly wiped the tears from Elise's face.

Megan had met Chris that past summer, and she knew how happy he had made Elise. She thought there would never be a time Chris would hurt her like this.

"I guess I was wrong." she whispered to herself.

"Some time, somewhere, I'm going to see him again. When I do, He'll remember how he hurt Elise. He'll know pain, as she did. The next time around." Megan made a promise to herself that remained in her mind from then on.

On Thursday Chris received his ring from Elise, along with a letter.

The letter read:' My Dearest Chris, I received your letter on Tuesday. I am returning your ring as you asked. I have never felt hurt in my life as you have hurt me. I cannot just stop loving you, as you have apparently been able to do with me, but if you ever want to talk about us, I am here for you.'

'I thought of you last night as I was watching a medical program drama series on television. The situation reminded me of the chasm that exists between us now. The doctor had fallen in love with a patient who was terminally ill. He deeply loved her and wanted to be with her, no matter how long they would have together. Toward the end of the program, the doctor faces his Love, and explains how much she means to him. He has too return to the hospital to perform surgery and tells her that he will be back to get her after he completes the surgery. Then they would leave together, to have a life together, to be together for as long as they have.'

When he does return to her home, there was a note on her door addressed to him from his Love.

'My Dearest; I'm afraid that I must leave you. I cannot put you through watching me ebb away into the Final Sleep. I know how much you love me, I know that I deeply, deeply, love you. When you think of me, think of that one poem I shared with you, that one part of the poem, for it is most appropriate now.' It is night, I am in my room, I am alone, and I am crying, for you are so far away, and I miss you and love you so very, very much...Your Everlasting Love.' 'In the final scene, the doctor is looking towards the sky at a plane flying into the clouds and disappearing.'

'I pray there will never be a time when a plane I'm on disappears into the clouds without you beside me.'

'I will always be here for you, Chris ... Your Everlasting Love, Elise.... Your Angel

Chapter 10
The Wrong Choice

It wasn't long before Chris realized that staying with Taylor was an error in judgment. They continued seeing each other, and they DID go to the Homecoming Dance. Taylor started getting more and more attention from upperclassman, in particular, Dan Bodner, and appeared to be enjoying the attention. Dan worked the same shift that Taylor and Chris did in the cafeteria. It seemed that anytime Chris was around, Dan would go out of his way to interact with Taylor, which he knew aggravated Chris. He knew Chris had that jealous side to him, the one nerve that he could step on that brought Chris's immaturity to the surface, and he would react to it. Taylor seemed to always brush it off as mere flirtation.

What finally put an end to it all was the day Chris came in to work late from class, and found Taylor crying in the back of the kitchen. Chris went over to her and asked what happened.

"It was Dan." she replied, through the tears.

"We were in the storage room getting supplies, when he grabbed me from behind, turned me toward him, and fondled my breasts and tried to kiss me"

Pure rage kicked in on Chris! He totally lost it!

"Where is he?! I'll kill him!!"

"He's still back in the supply closet. Please, Chris, let it go! Think of the consequences!" Taylor cried to Chris.

Taylor grabbed Chris's arm to stop him, but he tore away from her, with scratches down arms as he went, from her fingernails.

Jack entered the supply room in the back of the kitchen, where Dan was loading potatoes into the storage bin, his back toward Chris. There was a large kitchen knife next to the sacks that was used to open the sacks of potatoes.

Chris picked up the knife, and rammed into him from behind with his body, knocking Dan off his feet. As quickly as he hit the ground, Chris was on top of him, grabbing the front of his shirt and twisting it, holding the knife down by his side, and finally raising it toward Dan's neck.

"You bought it this time, Dan! This time you've pushed me to far!"

Dan turned pale! The expression on Dan's face was one that Chris would never forget. Dan cowered, not knowing what would happen to him next.

"Please, Chris," Dan cried, "I'm sorry, Honest! Please don't hurt me with that knife! I won't go near Taylor again! I promise!"

By this time, Taylor had entered the room and was pulling Chris off Dan as best she could.

"Stop, Chris! Stop this! Please, let him go! It isn't worth it!"

Somehow, someway, those words hit the right part of Chris's brain that put him back in control of himself.

"Okay, Okay, I'll stop. Don't you EVER touch her again, Dan!"

"You won't get away with it if it happens again!"

Chris was shaking and sweating as he backed away from Dan. He had never attacked anyone before. He didn't like the feeling surging through him. He lived with that feeling the rest of his life. He had just learned an important life lesson.

Taylor and Chris left the storage room and walked back over to Statler Dormitory to make sure they both calmed down.

Chris went home the next weekend, and didn't bother telling his parents what happened. Chris spent the weekend by himself, trying to figure where his relationship with Taylor was going. She seemed to become more distant, and acted like being with him was 'an obligation', not something that they should cherish together.

They spent time together, but the passion they shared before was gone. By the end of the semester, Chris's grades were at rock bottom, and their relationship was rapidly coming to an end.

Taylor stayed at Chris's home for a week at the end of the semester, and returned to New York on a Wednesday night bus. He took her to the bus station, and their 'Good-by' was brief. Then there was nothing. It was over.

As Chris drove back home from the terminal, he thought about Elise, and what she had said in her letter to him.

Chris called her as soon as he got home, and asked if he could see her at the Student Nurses Dormitory that Friday. To his delight, she said 'yes'. By this time, Elise and Chris had returned to seeing each other from time to time.

Chris went straight to his dad and asked him if he could use the car Friday night to see Elise.

"Wait a minute, Chris, I thought you were seeing that other girl that just went back to New York."

"You don't understand, Dad," he replied, "It's complicated." Chris went out on the side porch to think about what he was going to say to Elise. Any time Chris was going to see her, he always had a scenario figured out in his head. If that didn't work out, there was always a 'Plan B'... Don't misunderstand... Chris just didn't want to be without something to say.

Chapter 11

The Second Chance

Two days dragged by, and finally Friday night came. It was a beautiful evening, and Chris drove over to see Elise with the top down on his dad's convertible. He parked in the nurse's parking lot, and walked up the long walk to the nurse's dorm. He asked the girl at the front desk to call Elise's room. She arrived in the resident's lounge about 5 minutes later, still wearing her striped student nurse's uniform and her cap. She walked over to him, and embraced him.

"I'm glad to see you, Chris. It's been a long time." she said, smiling.

"I'm sorry I'm not in my regular clothes, but we had to stand in on a special orthopedic surgery procedure that didn't finish until six-thirty. I had to change out of my scrubs after surgery, and got back here as soon as I could."

They sat on one of the couches and just looked at each other as they talked.

Chris told her that he wasn't going back to college because his grade GPA was 0.9, and he had received a letter from the academic dean asking him to please not return! (Elise covered her mouth with her hand, so he couldn't see her laughing.)

After talking for about an hour, Chris got up to leave. He knew she was on Stand-by Call at the hospital.

"Well," Chris began, "Thanks for seeing me. I've really enjoyed talking and being with you.

Chris looked at Elise the way he had not so long ago, and the words 'I love you' were on his mind.

"I've missed you, Elise. Do you think we could do this again? I know your schedule at the hospital is getting tighter, but maybe we can get together some Friday."

"I've enjoyed it to, Chris. That would be nice."

Chris took her one hand in his hand, as they walked toward the door. Chris squeezed her hand slightly. She turned her head towards Chris, smiled, her hand squeezing back.

"Friday's may be a little impossible in June, Chris. I have floor duty on the afternoon shift most of the Fridays. The one evening I do have off is the third Saturday of June. It's the night of the Nurse's Ball at the College House." She left that statement hanging as they walked, to see how Chris would react.

Chris didn't know HOW to react to that. He forgot about 'Plan B', and was rapidly trying to figure a way to ask her to the ball.

"Who are you going with, if you don't mind my asking?" Chris asked, regaining his composure as quickly as he could.

"Well, I probably won't be going. Besides, no one has asked me."

There was Chris's opening to spend a night with his Forever Love.

"Well, if you wouldn't mind, I'd like to take you. I mean, if you're comfortable with it."

Elise hesitated for a moment, then looked down.

"I…" Elise paused for a bit. "I don't know Chris. We've had some heavy history between us. It may not be the best idea."

Elise wanted in her heart of hearts for Chris to ask her to the ball, but he would have to 'work' for it.

Chris was hoping she would say she would attend the ball with him.

Elise thought for a moment, then responded.

"Why don't you call me next Friday, and I'll let you know then."

That was Elise. She'd let him sweat it out for a while before she said 'yes'. He didn't care. Whatever it took, he wanted to be on the dance floor with her in his arms the night of the ball.

"Sure", Chris replied. "You think it over, and expect that call next Friday."

They stopped at the door leading to the outside. Chris placed his hands in hers and looked down into her eyes. He had forgotten how beautiful she really was, how much he really loved her.

"Good night, Elise. Thanks again for seeing me tonight."

Chris didn't want to leave.

She just squeezed his hands.

"See you around. Don't forget to call me." she said as she turned and walked towards the staircase which lead to the upper floors.

Chris watched her walk up the steps to the second-floor landing, thinking, 'Come on, now, turn around slightly and show me that beautiful smile. Make me happy.' (She looked back, just for a second, and she WAS smiling as she looked back!), Chris knew from that glance back that he would be with her at the ball.

Chris's dad was in the living room watching the television when he arrived home.

"Dad, don't make any plans three Saturdays from now. I'm going to the Nurse's Ball with Elise"

His dad just looked up at Chris and shook his head.

"I can't keep up with you, son, without a score card. First it was Elise, then Taylor, and now Elise again. Can't you just pick one, so I'm not confused." his dad said, trying to figure out something that Chris wasn't sure of himself.

"Okay. I guess I can stay home that night with your mother."

Chris thanked his dad, and went up to his room and prepared for bed.

Chris called Elise the following Friday, and she said that she had thought it over, and she would go to the ball with him.

They talked for about fifteen minutes, and then she had to get back to her studies. Before she hung up, she said she was looking forward to the ball, and would be ready about seven o'clock that evening.

"I'll see you then, Angel." Chris responded. He called her 'Angel' without thinking about it! He wasn't sorry he said it. it was so natural when they were a couple. Elise liked hearing Chris's nick-name for her. She didn't say anything, but she was pleased to hear that name again.

Chapter 12

The Nurse's Ball

Chris arrived at the nurse's dorm at exactly seven o'clock the Saturday night of the Ball. He had parked the car, walked up the walkway to the front door, into the alcove, and told the young lady at the desk to call Elise's room.

"She'll be right down, sir." The young lady told him as she hung up the phone.

Megan, Elise's roommate, was helping her finish getting dressed, and putting the final touches on her gown. Megan thought Elise looked so beautiful.

"Are you sure about this, Elise? I'm afraid you're just going to get hurt again." Megan said with some concern, as she adjusted the gown.

Elise just looked in to the mirror as she finished her make-up.

"Am I sure that I still love Chris? Yes. Am I sure that tonight is going to bring us back to where we once were? I don't know. I just want to go to the ball, and be 'Cinderella' tonight. I want to be in Chris's arms, holding him close to me, and dancing like we did not too long ago. I want to be on that 'Cloud 9' everyone talks about, feeling loved as I was before."

Megan hugged Elise, as a small tear was shed for her friend.

“Have a good time, Elise.” Megan managed to say before Elise went through the bedroom door, walked down the hall, and down the steps to meet Chris.

Chris was standing at the bottom of the steps. Elise stopped for a moment, then descended the staircase with the grace of a princess. She had her auburn hair up in a twist. Her smile brightened her countenance. She was wearing a single diamond on a chain, and the gold chain shown as the light reflected off the diamond. The diamond sparkled, sending rays of light back toward their original source.

Her dress was a three-quarter shoulder length white chiffon, with a white chiffon wrap around her exposed shoulders. On her feet, she had what Chris called ‘Cinderella shoes’ (glass-looking slippers). Tonight, she was truly Chris’s angel.

She reached the bottom of the staircase, looked in to his eyes (his jaw had dropped open!) and asked,” What do you think, Chris? Do I meet with your approval?”

They gazed at each other as their inner selves exchanged the heart felt fantasia that was their love.

“...... Elise, you will be the most beautiful lady at the ball tonight. Thank you for being with me.”

They drove for about forty-five minutes to the College House. Most of the nurses had arrived already with their dates. They went up the stairs from the parking lot and entered the building, and walked over to the ballroom. Elise gently took Chris’s hand and lead him over to a table where two of her friends were sitting with their dates. Introductions were made, and the night began.

The six of them had a fantastic time the entire night. They laughed and talked, and shared experiences. The best time of the evening, for them, was when Elise and Chris danced together. They danced close to each other, her head resting on his chest, just like when they were first dating. Every once and a while, Chris would pull her a little closer and gently kiss her cheek. She would pull away, slightly, and return the kiss.

Chris and Elise floated the whole evening on the cloud of fantasy that was theirs alone.

As always, time was running as fast as it could, and the evening was coming to an end. The freshman nursing students had a curfew of midnight, so they had to leave the ball.

Chris and Elise walked down to the car, Chris opened the door, and Elise got in. He went around to the other side and got into the driver's seat. They just sat there for a moment, not saying anything, just staring at each other. The words 'I love you' were on both of their minds and lips, but the words were never said. This would have been a second chance for both, but neither said those words that would have healed them both.

"You want to know something, Elise? I can't remember having such a wonderful time with you. Was tonight real, or were we living in a dream?"

"You tell me, Chris, I feel the same way you do."

Chris reached over and placed his hand in hers, looking longingly into her eyes. Nothing was said. They just shared their feelings through their eyes, moving back and forth between their souls. So much had happened between them, but neither of them would be strong enough to say, "I love you".

As Chris drove back to the nurse's dorm, he let his mind wonder to the past, to the times they shared together, the times they sought safe harbor from the storms of turmoil in their lives, to the rejuvenation of their love, to all those things that brought beauty to the essence of their being, to times when it was just Chris and Elise.

Chris drove into the parking lot across from the dorm, and shut the engine off. He turned and looked at Elise. Chris had a small tear slowly moving down his cheek because he was bursting in his heart. Chris hoped Elise didn't notice.

"May I kiss you good-night, Elise?" he asked.

The look on Elise's face changed. He could tell he had hurt her by asking.

"Do you really think you have to ask?" she replied.

She was quietly crying, as he took her in his arms, and their lips met. Would one of them say 'I love you', and things would once again be right between them? When that soft kiss ended, he wanted to say so much to her.

"Elise…" Chris began, but she stopped him.

"I… I don't want you to say anything right now, Chris. I just want to take this night back to my room and fall asleep in the fantasy we shared at the ball tonight. I want to drift off and whatever we had this night will be remembered in my dreams. Now, please walk me to the dorm."

They got out of the car, and walked up to the front door. They held each other once more, and kissed briefly.

"Good night, Elise."

"Good night, Chris.", was all she said to him, then turned and walked into the dorm. She wanted so much to tell Chris she was still in love with him, but the time didn't seem right. She would have to wait.

Chris stood there and watched her walk up to the second floor and disappear. This time, she did not look back. Perhaps more time was needed. Chris just stood there for a moment, staring up at the empty hall on the second floor. He wanted to call to her, to bring her back, to be his love, his life, his 'Breath Away', but it was not to be.

Chapter 13

USAF Tour of Duty

The summer was going by quickly, and Chris couldn't find a job. Since he couldn't return to college, and the military draft was in full swing, his mother suggested that he try the Air Force and see what it had to offer.

He went over to Washington, Pennsylvania US Air Force recruiter the second week in July, and ended up signing on for four years. After all the paperwork and physical, in August 1962, he was on his way to Lackland Air Force Base in San Antonio Texas. He was sworn in at 1600 hours that day, and was on the plane to Texas at 1900 hours.

Talk about a rude awakening! The first thing Chris learned, after he fell out of the bus at Lackland, is that the drill instructors were not nice to you.

No matter what you said, it was wrong.

No matter how you tried to stand at attention it was not right.

You had ABSOLUTELY no opinion that could be expressed.

You, for all intent and purposes were the world's greatest loser!

Chris and the rest of the recruits were marched to their squadron barracks and assigned their bunks. They had been told to only bring enough change of clothes for three days in a small gym bag. All seventy-two of them had to stand by their bunks at attention after they dumped the contents of the gym bags out on the bed. What some of the guys brought with them besides clothes was amazing!

One guy, Nick Harding, had a stack of Playboy magazines, a picture of his sixty-five foot yacht, the 'Hearts of the Sea', a pair of his girlfriend's nylon stockings (worn at least once), and a pair of striped bikini bottoms. The drill instructor was not pleased.

"Where did you think you were coming to, boy? The Playboy mansion? and these panties? Think you might want to try them on and see if they fit you? If they do, you definitely AIN'T staying in MY Flight (a division of a squadron), I'll transfer your sorry butt to the WAF Squadron!.."

Nick was beet red as the verbal dressing down continued. Though he was about six-foot three inches tall, the drill instructor had reduced him to about six inches high, theoretically at least.

The drill instructor picked up the stockings with his riding crop, and placed them around Nick's neck, placed his face within an inch or two from Nick's face…

"Now put all these 'luxury items' back in that gym bag, and stand to!" he yelled. Just a side note:

Nick was the first man in the first squad in the Flight formation. Chris was the Guide-On Bearer (The Flight's ID banner) for the Flight and marched right in front of him. Two weeks after training began, Chris had blisters all over the back of his feet. Nick, being so tall, had a nasty habit of walking on the backs of Chris's combat boots. Chris asked him several times to stop, but Nick told him to make his strides longer.

One day about half-way through the third week, the Flight was over on the parade field doing close order drills, and Nick hit the back of Chris's one foot, and then the same on the other. Chris had had it! He ran forward about ten feet, turned 180 degrees, lowered the guide-on, and ran headlong at Nick. Chris looked like a British Bengal Lancer, as he aimed the blunt point directly at Nick's stomach! Fortunately, Nick moved to the side, and the silver point of the guide-on hit him on his side, and down he went. Chris dropped the guide-on, jumped on Nick, and began to pummel him.

The drill instructor was on Chris before he knew it, and he was pulled off.

Chris had to stand extra duty, was removed as guide-on bearer, and had to do extra PT, but Nick never bothered him after that, so it was worth the consequences Chris received!

The first three days, roll call was at 0430 hours. The "Rainbows", as the new recruits were called because of the different colored clothes they wore when they arrived at Basic Training, had to be up, dressed, and ready for inspection by 0500 hours. Then it was over to the chow hall where they were given ten minutes to eat. They ate so quickly that their stomach began digestion ten minutes after the food had already reached the small intestine. Then, it was march over to the Physical Training field for an hour or two of push-ups, running in place, sit-ups, mile runs around the track, etc. Then, it was back to the barracks for a shower, back into fatigue uniforms. Afterwards, they marched over to either the Administration Building to fill out paperwork, TOLD they WOULD write home by tomorrow and let Their families know they arrived safely and were doing fine. Or, depending on the day, they marched over to the Hospital Clinic area for various shots and vaccinations.

Finally, on the third day, they marched over to Supply and were issued their uniforms, which they had to tag with their stamp that was given to them that had their name and serial number on it. Then, they had to march back to the squadron barracks and set up their lockers and closets according to USAF regulations.

Training continued. At the beginning of the fifth week, they went to the rifle range for 3 days.

The first 2 days dealt with learning every aspect of the M-1 rifle, how to take it apart, and reassemble it, how to clean it, and how to hold it in the various positions for firing. They also went through what was known as 'dry fire' – no ammunition was utilized, just training and acting as if they were in an actual firefight, utilizing the positions they would be firing in.

Day 3, the Flight went to the rifle range for live fire on targets set at fifty yards. This is where the safety training with the M-1 was put into play. The drill instructor stressed the M-1 was to be carried with the muzzle pointing straight in the air. At no time was it to be lowered unless it was to target shoot or to kill.

Seventy-two men lined up on the firing line, in the standing position, and were given two ten round ammo clips with live ammo.

Safety demanded an immediate cease fire if an individual's weapon jammed or misfired, making sure the safety was on, and the weapon was still facing down range. The individual would raise one hand and the drill instructor would clear the problem.

Chris was the tenth man on the line. The seventh man had a shell casing jam on his second shot. Instead of following safety protocol, the airman left the safety off, swung the weapon to the right, and yelled, "My gun's jammed, Sargent." An immediate cease fire was called for the whole line by the Weapons Range Sargent, and the drill instructor told the airman with the jam to set the weapon on the v-shaped locking block on the ground. Once the weapon was locked in the block, the drill instructor kicked it with his boot, and eight rounds went down range.

"Do you see why we have safety protocol?" the drill instructor yelled at the individual. "You could have killed at least four men by your lack of safety."

Chris was in the third man position. He would have been killed. Another life lesson hit him square in the face. Life or death can be just a breath away.

After finishing training on the rifle range, Chris and his Flight trained on the Combat Obstacle Course. There, they were subjected to mine fields with live charges constantly exploding around them, obstacles that had to be climbed, live fire above them as they maneuvered through a stretch of ground with barbed wire above them, repelling down a hillside using ropes and carabineers, then ran for about one hundred feet, and had to do a hand-over-hand overhead bars across a creek, with explosions going on all around them, all with full packs, helmets, and their M1 rifles. The final obstacle was the rope slide.

They had to cross a fifty-foot span of stagnant water, twenty feet in the air, with the rope at an angle of about fifty degrees… Chris hated heights, but he somehow managed to complete the course because if he didn't, he would have two additional weeks of training tacked on to his basic training… There was no way he was going through that again!

Basic Training finally ended the last of September,1962, and Chris received his orders transferring him to Keesler Air Force, at Biloxi, Mississippi, to train as an airborne radar technician and electronics specialist. He also received a sealed set of orders that he was to turn over to his squadron commander at the base.

After a twelve hour bus ride from San Antonio, Texas, Chris and the other thirty recruits arrived at the base and were taken to a hanger which the base used as a processing center. Since it was so late in the evening, they bussed the recruits over to what they called the Triangle Area of the base, which contained the base barracks for the Electronics Training airmen.

The following morning, they were bussed back to the hanger and processed in, getting barrack assignments, mail room box assignments, and told that since the next class didn't start until the end of October, they would have a barracks chief brief them on the day's assignments every day until classes began. Things went well the first ten days, and then on October 14, 1962, the whole base was put on alert. A growing confrontation was brewing between the United States, Russia, and Cuba over nuclear missiles Russia had secretly placed on Cuban soil. The United States thought there were only 2-3 ICBMs on the island, but history showed there were 34 ICBMs.

President John F. Kennedy and Premier Nikita Khrushchev were about to push the famous 'Red Button' in each of their countries over the missiles in Cuba.

Each one was trying to see if the other would 'blink', and back down. President Kennedy held fast, made a deal with Khrushchev, and the crisis was finally over in November, as missiles from Cuba were dismantled and returned to the Soviet Union.

Chapter 14

The Cuban Missile Crisis

During the week of October 14, 1962, while waiting to start class, the barracks bay was assigned night guard duty on the Biloxi beaches, just two blocks from the base, across from US Highway 90.

They were bussed over to the base armory, and issued M1 rifles, and several ammo clips, which were empty! The OIC (Officer in Charge) briefed them on the situation.

"Men, each of you is going to patrol a section of beach about 300 feet long. You will have your weapons slung, and not in a threatening position. You will continue the patrol until properly relieved. If you see anything that looks like a beach landing, you will immediately inform your squad leader by radio which we have also issued. They, in turn will contact the base and the Air Police will meet you at your deployment area and then you will be issued live ammunition for your clips, and proceed with wartime protocol on the beach."

Chris didn't believe what he was hearing! No ammo. Call back to the base if you see anything? Who was running this show?!! Here he is, about to be caught up in a hostile beach landing with foreign nationals and no ammo!

Chris put up his hand.

"Pardon me, Sir, but why aren't we being issued live ammo in the first place?", he asked.

"Because, airman, this is a tourist town, and the Air Force doesn't want you taking shots at anything that moves or lands on the beach. We'll be able to back you up quickly from here, if need be. What we want to show is a strong military presence."

They got into the trucks, and were taken to their deployment sites on the beach. Chris got out of the truck at his deployment site, slung his rifle over his shoulder, and began patrolling the stretch of 300 feet he was assigned. He noticed that most of the beach was clear, except a few teenagers, and the airmen had orders to ask them to return to their homes.

Chris walked back and forth in his fatigues and combat helmet for about four hours. In some ways, he was scared to death, as he looked down towards the darkened water as it lapped at the shore. In other ways, he really felt like a 'warrior', if you would, defending his country.

Chris was finally relieved, and returned to the barracks. He slept a little longer the next day because he had foot patrol duty.

Chapter 15

Permanent Station Assignment

Chris's airborne electronics training finished about a year later. The sealed orders that he brought with him to Keesler Air Force Base were then opened and activated, assigning him to a top-secret base in Arizona to begin working on a new defense initiative known as SDI (Strategic Defense Initiative). His job was going to be in research and development, along with trouble-shooting the electronic phases of a joint NASA and US Air Force project called 'The 4 Apostles '. The project was to be in three phases.

The first phase was the research and development into the feasibility of such a First Strike platform and evaluation of its target accuracy. Instead of utilizing missiles, an argon blue laser was activated towards a predetermined target, thus eliminating nuclear fallout produced from a nuclear explosion.

The second phase would be the full assembly of the platform, testing the components on the ground and studying the results of the tests.

The third and final phase would be the placement of these platform stations in space, once the ground testing was complete. The platforms would then be tested on remote islands in the Pacific Ocean.

The public was never told about this project, due to its nature and sensitivity, as well as the national security concerns.

The project involved the use of four laser platforms in space, armed with high yield cobalt blue lasers. Once in orbit, these platforms could be tasked to position inside their geosynchronous orbits to any configuration the Command and Control Centers on Earth wished. What was NOT known is that the United States and Israel would share control of the satellite laser stations. This type of defense agreement with Israel was never made public.

The idea was that by positioning the lasers, tactical surgical strikes could be achieved without the use of troops or occupying foreign soil.

Though this was not an open deterrent to nuclear war, it was one that offered tactical options without the devastation of an atomic or hydrogen bomb.

While Chris was involved with the R & D, He was also trained in Advanced Medical Laboratory procedures. Some of the items that the personnel handled required monitoring medically as a safety precaution.

Chris finished his part of the R&D project, and was given a 30 day leave. Chris was flown back from the 'Area 51' base, as he called it, in a C-135 cargo jet – once again, no windows. A lot had transpired in his Air Force life, but there was no way he could discuss it. Flying back to Pittsburgh, Chris tried to figure out how he was going to explain to Elise what he was going to do next.

Chris called Elise a day after he returned home to Washington, Pennsylvania, and asked if she could see him that Friday during the day. She said she would be able to, and asked where they were going.

"South View Park," he answered.

She seemed happy with that. There was a little bridge they would visit from time to time in the middle of a grove in the middle of the park. The grove was a bit off the main road, and half-way hidden.

Chris picked Elise up at her nursing dorm about 10 AM and they drove to their little hide away, parked the car, and walked down to the bridge, holding hands and Elise putting her head on Chris's shoulder.

Elise stopped by the tree at the beginning of the bridge, let his hand go, and leaned against the tree, turning her head to the side and looking at him.

"What is it, Chris? What is it that's bothering you? We only come here if there is something on your mind."

Chris stared out over the park, not knowing what to say first.

Chris was half-way across the tiny bridge, and was holding on to the side rail. He walked back over to Elise, and they embraced, holding each other tightly.

"Chris, please tell me what's wrong. We've always worked things out before."

Chris pulled away slightly.

"The Air Force has assigned me to a facility that is classified. No one I know is to know it's location, or what my job will be. I'll be gone about a year. I can have no communications with you. If you want to write to me, I'll give you a PO Box number, which is here in Pittsburgh, but I won't be able to read them until my assignment is complete, and I have returned to Pittsburgh."

He reached into his jacket pocket, and pulled out a set of instructor's wings. While he was in training, he was asked to be an instructor to bring other personnel up to speed who were having difficulties on the theory and concepts of the project, and who needed additional training on troubleshooting the guidance and rotational control systems of the platform. Chris wanted her to have his wings. It was a pair of wings with a torch between them, signifying the torch of knowledge. Of all the things Chris did in the Air Force, earning his wings was the most fulfilling.

He wanted her to have something that was important to him while he was away. Wearing his wings, he hoped Elise would think about them and their relationship. Chris loved her more than anyone else. He hoped he wouldn't lose her.

She turned to him, and he held her in his arms. Chris placed the wings on her jacket, and lovingly looked in to her eyes.

"Elise, every airman who has ever earned his wings who has had someone they cared for deeply, pinned their wings on the person they cared for the most. I'd like you to wear my wings. Someday, you'll have something to wear in addition to my wings, a ring on your finger."

Elise had surmised that there was going to be a long time before they would see each other again as Jack pinned them to her jacket. Elise gently ran her fingers over the wings and torch and the scrolled wording below them which said 'Instructor'.

"I don't know what to say, Chris. I've never been pinned before, Of course, I'll wear them."

She put her hand into her coat pocket, and pulled out a piece of paper.

"I thought this was going to happen, Chris, you, being away for a long time. I wrote this for you, for us, last night." she said, handing him the paper.

Chris looked down at the poem she had written, remembering they used to visit this place in the autumn because of the beautiful foliage. Chris read it quietly to himself:

Fall Enchantment

The sun came searching for us,
Burning away the morning mist that hid us from its view...
We fled to the protective autumn woods...
Our golden sanctuary from reality...
Discontent... the sun sent peering shafts of light
Through the leafy boughs ... and found us,
Lost in each other's eyes...
Like the sun... I too, was discontent...
Until you!...

"Elise, this is so beautiful." Chris whispered softly in her ear.

They held each other, looking at the park around them and remembering. They stood on the bridge for a long time, and Elise reminded Chris of something which would pull at his heart.

"You know I'm dating now, Chris. Every once and a while, I need someone to just enjoy life with. Go to a movie, go out to dinner or dancing. Things that make life fun."

She was right. Chris couldn't expect her to wait around for him, especially since he was gone for long periods of time. Then there was the security issue. He couldn't tell her anything about his assignment.

"I know, Elise. If I could change things I would. You have the right to live your life your way. I understand."

They kissed once more, then left the little bridge in the park and headed back to the car. He drove her to her dorm, but this time it was Chris who was hurting inside. He couldn't reconcile in his mind her being with someone else. Things being what they were, there was nothing he could do.

After leaving her at the nurse's dorm, Chris rode around, thinking and wondering how their lives would turn out, then headed to his home in Washington.

Leave time went faster than ever, and Chris didn't get a chance to see Elise before he left for his new base assignment.

The night before he left, he sat in the study in his home and composed a poem for Elise, and mailed it to her dormitory at the hospital. It was something for her to look at from time to time. and ponder their love:

Autumn Rapsody
Rustling Leaves – you hear them there -
In the cool, crisp autumn air?
Woodland creatures scurrying, too –
Playing there in front of you...
A rustic bridge where you once stood
so lost in love, within the wood, -

The trees which sheltered both of you,
Aflame once more with colored hue.

The zephyrs – cool – caress your face,
As you recall a fond embrace,
And as you walk upon the dew,
Sweet moments now come back to you.

What was in that autumn day,
That made it right in every way?
Was it touch… or smile… or eyes
Or secret dreams within your sighs?

Was it perhaps an outstretched hand,
Or whispered words – "I understand"
That made you feel a woman true,
Because he loved… and wanted … You!

The next chapter in Chris's life had begun, with things still unsettled between Elise and him.

Chapter 16

A Surprise from the Past

About two years had passed, and Chris was sent TDY (Temporary Duty Assignment) to Keesler Air Force Base to assist in the hospital laboratory and the emergency room, due to lack of personnel at the hospital. Since he had completed his part in the laser project, he was able to assist as a medic.

Chris was working the ER on a Friday, when the Emergency Alert system received a call for flight line support for incoming wounded from Viet Nam, eight of which were ICU patients. An airman by the name of Lance Brennen was Chris's partner on cases in the ER, so they both headed for the first Ready Alert Ambulance in the ambulance parking area.

"Did the dispatcher say how many patients are inbound?" Lance asked, as he drove out of the parking area.

"Twenty patients, eight are ICU critical cases. They'll be accompanied by combat nurses. The rest have corpsman assigned to them. Since we'll be the first on the ramp to meet the Angel Flight, we'll start taking the ICU cases."

They were waiting on the ramp when the first C-130 landed. The aircraft taxied across the field to the processing area which had been set up, and the critical patients were moved from the aircraft to the waiting ambulances. Lance and Chris were in a high-boy ambulance, and could take four of the ICU patients with them. Some were on ventilators, some had chest tubes to prevent lungs from collapsing, trauma collars to stabilize the cervical spine. You name the body trauma, they had it. Once they were aboard the ambulance, and the combat nurses had them stabilized for the ride to the base hospital, they proceeded carefully back to the hospital.

Receiving trauma specialists were waiting at the ambulance entrance, and carefully removed the patients from the ambulance. These patients were then taken to a special care unit the hospital administration had set up to take on the extra load. Some of the patients had to be isolated because of certain diseases encountered in battlefield areas.

After Lance and Chris had assisted the specialist teams with the triage, they headed back to the ER. Senior Corpsman Bill Stracka met them as they approached the doors to the ER.

"Airman Logan." he called out.

"Yes, Sir." Chris answered.

"One of the combat nurses – a captain - that flew in with that first Angel Flight wants to see you in the visitor's lounge. She says she knows you from Pittsburgh"

Chris searched his brain 'Who could she be? I know a lot of nurses, but I don't know any serving in 'Nam.'

Chris went to the visitor lounge. It was empty with one exception, a pony-tailed, fatigue uniformed, five-foot six red haired captain. She had her back to Chris as he entered the room.

"You wanted to see me, Captain?" he asked.

She turned and faced him.

"Yes, Airman Logan, I certainly do. I promised myself that if I ever saw you again, I would give you something to remember."

With that, she slapped Chris as hard as she could across the face, knocking him into a chair.

"Captain," Chris said as he up righted himself in the chair. "Pardon me, Captain, but who are you, and what did I do?.."

With her hands on her hips, she leaned over him. Chris didn't know what to expect next.

"Does the name Megan Stern mean anything to you? I was Elise Hunter's roommate in nurse's training. We met at Seaton Hill. You, Chris, are a coward! You didn't have the decency to break her heart face-to-face. You had to send her a 'Dear John' letter. She was hysterical when she got it, then about destroyed the room before falling asleep on top of the bed coverings she had thrown on the floor. I swore if I ever ran into you again, you would feel pain like Elise did that day."

Megan's green eyes were still flaring as Chris rose from the chair and came to attention.

"The captain is right, mam. I was exactly what you said, a coward. Elise deserved better than that. I apologized to her, face-to- face, and now I apologize to you for being such a coward. Please forgive me."

Megan just shook her head and looked at the floor. She was still upset. Chris had never had a friend he was that close to, and he felt he had betrayed Megan as well.

Megan pulled her head back, said nothing, turned, and left the room still shaking her head.

Lance came in as Megan left and noticed the red slap mark on Chris's face.

"Are you all right, Chris?" He asked, "What was that all about?"

"Yeah, Lance. I'm all right. It was a long time coming and something I fully deserved."

No incident report was filed.

Chris's time at Kessler Air Force Base ended about a month later, and he returned to the 'Area 51' base. Lance and Chris had become good friends and they decided to keep in touch.

One year later, he was discharged from the Air Force and returned to his home in Pennsylvania.

Right after Chris landed at Pittsburgh International Airport, in a windowless C-135, he went to the base headquarters building to pick up any mail that he had received. There was only one letter, and it had Elise's address in the upper left-hand corner of the envelope. He sat down on a bench just outside the headquarters building, and opened the letter. As he read the letter, his gut slowly knotted up, and a profound sense of loss came over him. The letter contents were as follows:

'My Dearest Chris,

'This will be my last letter to you. Please try to understand.'

'It is night, I am in my room, I am alone, and I am crying, because you are so far away, and because I love you so very much. Your Everlasting Love…'

'Do you remember those words, Chris? They were in a letter I wrote to you when you were trying to figure out who was most important in your life. I had hoped it would be me, but, it wasn't.

When your situation with Taylor didn't work out, you returned to me. You and I continued seeing each other, but our relationship was guarded, and neither of us would totally recommit.

I thought the night of the Nurse's Ball, we would restore what we had together. Everything seemed so right with us that night, but, again, neither of us gave way. Perhaps it was for the best, I don't know. I remembered a part of a poem I once read, and the words hold meaning for me now.

'Life isn't about waiting for the storm to pass, it's about learning to dance in the rain.

It isn't about what anyone else thinks, because it is you who will think for yourself... And it's you who will run your own life'.

As I told you, I had been dating, and was dating Bill Potter, Mary Lynne's ex, for a long time. He

> told me that he loved me, and wanted to marry me and take me to Arizona with him on his new job. I'll admit that I hesitated because I still have feelings for you. However, I said 'yes', and we will be married and gone by the time you receive this letter.
>
> It is time we both moved on with our lives. I want stability in my life. I want to have a husband who comes home to me every night, tells me he missed me, tells me he loves me. I want children I can raise and enjoy the time of parenthood. I want all these things. I wanted them with you, but it will never be. Please forgive me. I hope you think of me from time to time. Remember us together. And, in a tiny space in your heart, keep those memories. Continue to hold me and love me.'
>
> Perhaps sometime in the future, you will be somewhere and see a girl in a white chiffon dress and 'Cinderella shoes', her auburn hair in a twist, a single diamond suspended from a gold chain around her neck. Don't hesitate this time, Chris. Go to her. She will turn her head slightly to the right, and say, 'Miss me?' You will take her in your arms, tell her you love her, and know you will never miss her again. All my love… Your Everlasting Love, your Angel, Elise…'

The letter was post marked three months prior. Chris read and reread the letter as he sat there, his inner self becoming void, as a gentle breeze brushed by his face, forcing him to realize his Forever Love had chosen another path of life to travel. Soon the pages of the letter were moistened with tears, causing the ink to fade on the words they touched. Elise had moved on. Now it was his time to move on. Alone.

Chapter 17

De'ja' vu

Elise and Bill were married on June 10th, about three months before Jack returned to Pittsburgh. After they returned from their honeymoon in Florida, they moved out to Tucson, Arizona. Bill was assigned to a company that was working on classified government projects on the outskirts of the city, and Elise got a job in a local orthopedic hospital as an OR scrub nurse. After a few months, things seemed to settle down in Elise's life, she liked her job in the OR, and eventually became a chief scrub nurse.

Bill arrived home one night with some news that would affect Elise, but she would not become aware of the ramifications of the news until sometime later.

"Hi, Honey. Your husband's home," Bill said as he entered the house, closed the door behind him, and tossed his suit jacket over the back of the living room chair. Elise was in the kitchen fixing dinner.

"I'm in the kitchen, Bill," she answered, "How was your day?"

Bill walked back to kitchen, and grabbed an apple out of the bowl on the sink.

"Guess what, Elise? I've been picked to head a special project for the military. It seems like they've been working on it for the past four years, and they're ready for the test trials. It's all 'hush-hush'. I even have to go through a special top-secret security clearance to be on the project."

'*Now where have I heard that before*?' she thought.

She had never told Bill about Chris's work while he was in the Air Force. Information about where he was and what he was doing was never disclosed. Was she going to have to contend with this *again?*

"You're not going to have to move, or go to some secret base, are you?" Elise asked, staring down into the kitchen sink, her back still towards Bill. She felt a chill travel up her spine.

"Don't tell me I'm going to have to go through this nightmare again."

"Naw." Bill responded as he walked around to the other side of the kitchen sink, leaning over and kissing Elise on the cheek.

"There may be people from the FBI come around and question you. It's all just routine for this type of project."

Elise reached up and took plates off the shelf and placed them out on the dining room table.

"Is the FBI coming to the house? I really don't want them coming to the hospital, not to my workplace."

Elise was anxious over the thoughts of the government delving into her life. She had nothing to fear. It was just an annoying inconvenience she preferred not to deal with.

"What questions do you think they'll ask?", she asked as she continued to set the table for dinner.

Bill had gone into the living room, turned the TV on, and sat down in his chair.

"I don't know, Elise. I know they usually delve into your personal life, past and present. Who you have known through high school, college, nurses training. All of that. Then there's your present. Where you work, who you work with, how long you've known everybody in your life. You know, stuff like that. They'll be doing the same to me."

Elise put the dinner on the table and called Bill in to eat. There was very little talk that evening over dinner.

"I have to work the evening shift tomorrow, Bill. I'll have your supper in the oven. Is that okay with you?" Elise said as she cleared the table.

"Well, I would rather have you here with me, but I guess I can eat alone one night."

Elise cleaned up the dishes and went into the study while Bill stretched out on the couch and fell asleep watching the news on TV.

Elise started surfing the Web on the computer, to try and locate Chris. If the FBI was going to talk with her, they were probably going to talk with Chris also. She had no idea Chris had started back to college, and was headed for a career in medicine. She did find out where he was living, and his address via satellite photograph.

She had no computer address for him, but eventually found him on the freshman College Registry.

She started to write a letter to him to expect the FBI, but hesitated.

'No,' she thought, 'I'll just wait to see what they ask about our relationship, then I'll write him and let him know what they said'

Elise shut the computer off, and leaned back in the chair, thinking about Chris, and how much she missed him. But she was married to Bill now, and she was in this marriage for good. She left the study, gave Bill, who was still asleep on the couch, a nudge to wake him up, and climbed the stairs and went to their bedroom to prepare for bed.

Elise bathed, put on her negligée, and lay on the bed on her left side, and tried to go to sleep. A tear gently slipped from her eye, and moved down her cheek, and fell onto her pillow, where it disappeared into the linen.

Bill was still in the shower, and didn't hear what she whispered, as she drifted off to sleep.

"Good night, Chris. 'It is **night,** I am in my room, I am **alone,** and I am **crying, because I still love you, and miss you** so very much… Good night, **my Darling…**"

Chapter 18

The Investigation

The next day, about 10 AM, Elise had just finished cleaning the living room, and watering her plants, when the doorbell rang. Elise went to the front door and opened it. There stood two tall men in trench coats.

"May I help you, gentlemen?" she asked.

"Good morning, Mam, I'm Special Agent Taylor, and this is Special Agent Todd. We're with the FBI," as both gentleman showed her their badge and ID's.

"May we come in and speak with you?"

Elise showed some surprise, but she knew why they were there.

"Of course, please come in."

The men followed her into the living room, and sat on the couch. Elise sat in a chair opposite them.

"How can I help you?" Elise asked.

"As you know, your husband is slated to head a Department of Defense project, and is required to have a back-ground check, which includes his wife, and relatives." Special Agent Taylor explained.

"We have already started the back-ground check on your husband and you."

"When we were checking your back-ground, we found that you had a relationship with a Chris Logan. Is that true Mrs. Potter?"

Elise was taken back.

"Well, yes. We went together in high school and my first year of nurse's training, but I don't see how that's relative to what my husband will be doing," Elise said, trying to figure out what was going on.

"While you were at Bartlett Hospital School of Nursing, Chris Logan was attending Craig/Sanderson College, was he not?" Special Agent Todd asked.

"Yes", she replied, "He was majoring in Biology and Computer Science."

Special Agent Taylor was writing notes as Elise spoke, and asked another question.

"Did Chris ever mention to you a young lady he was seeing at the college by the name of Taylor Wagner?"

Now *that* was a name Elise wanted nothing to do with!

"I knew OF her. She was the reason Chris and I stopped seeing each other. Beside her being a tramp, and was from New York City, I can't tell you any more about her."

Taylor looked down at his notebook, and continued the questions.

"Did Chris ever mention any conversations he had with her?"

Elise was starting to feel uncomfortable.

"Whatever conversations he had with her, he knew better than to discuss them with me. The only conversation we had about her was when we discontinued our relationship."

"To your knowledge, did Chris ever go on any trips with her?"

Elise had had it." Look, this is a very sore subject with me, and it seems to me that you should be asking Chris these questions," she retorted.

"That's all we need right now," said Special agent Todd, "But we will be back if we need more information."

Elise just wanted them to leave.

"I have to get ready for my shift at the hospital, so if you gentleman don't mind, I'll show you to the door."

After the agents had left her house, Elise went upstairs to her bedroom, lay across the bed and cried. She couldn't stand the thought of rehashing the worst part of her life, losing the one she cared for the most.

Chapter 19

Problems with the Background Check

Elise went to the hospital that afternoon, but was noticeably shaken. Her best friend, Katie Wilson, noticed her demeanor as they were changing into the OR scrub uniforms.

"You alright, Elise?" she asked as she started putting on the insulated OR shoes.

Elise just stared down at the floor, folding her arms together.

"Just a bad day, Katie. I'll be all right" She said unconvincingly.

"I'll take this trauma case that's coming up from ER, if you want me to." Katie offered.

"No, Katie, I'll work it. I need to work to keep my mind occupied. I'll be okay. You take the next case," she insisted.

With that, Elise began scrubbing up in the Scrub Room just off the Operating Room.

Several weeks went by. Bill came home from work one day with some news about the background checks, and sounded depressed as he walked through the door and called for Elise.

"Elise? Where are you? I heard from the FBI today. It seems there is snag in the background checks."

Elise was changing into her jeans and shirt from her nursing uniform up in the bedroom.

"Hang on, Bill. I'll be right down," she replied, sliding into her slippers and heading toward the stairs.

She met Bill at the bottom of the staircase.

"What did the FBI say? Are they close to finishing the background checks?"

"Mine is done," Bill said, "It's yours that seems to be holding things up."

"Why?" she asked.

"It looks as if the problem is not with you, but with Chris," Bill replied as he entered the living room and sat in his chair.

"How is what Chris may have done have anything to do with me?"

"I don't know, Honey, but it seems like 'guilty through association'."

Elise pulled her legs up under her as she sat on the couch across from Bill.

"Why don't you call your dad, Elise, and see if he has any pull to get some answer for us. Wasn't he friends with that one guy that was in the FBI office in Pittsburgh. Maybe he can find something out."

Elise pondered the suggestion and agreed.

"Dad should be home any time now. I'll give him a call after we have dinner."

She made the call about six-thirty and talked with her father. He said he would make inquiries on the following day. Elise thanked him and asked him to call her back as soon as he knew something.

Two days passed, Elise was in her living room reading a book when the doorbell rang. She went to the door and opened it. It was another FBI Special Agent in a trench coat!

'My goodness, do these guys ever wear anything else but trench coats?' she thought to herself as she asked him in.

"Mrs. Potter, my name is Special Agent Jerry Winfield. I received a call from the Pittsburgh, PA office about a background check on you and your husband. Special Agent Phil Landsdale said he was a friend of your fathers, and as luck would have it, we were in a Navy SEAL team together. That's a special type of bond, Mrs. Potter. We always had each other's back. No request went unanswered. Even though this is completely off the record, I'm going to explain the situation to you. There is only one provision, that you must never speak of this to anyone, not even your husband, because if you do, you will be subject to a heavy fine and imprisonment and I'll be prosecuted, and sent to prison. Do you understand?"

Elise was taken back by that the last statement, but she wanted to know what was going on.

"Yes, of course. I just want to be done with this."

Agent Winfield leaned back in the chair and began the explanation.

"About ten years ago, the United States and Russia began getting real serious about nuclear war, and who, if anyone, would survive such a war. That's when the 'Balance of Power' really started.

Both sides needed to keep an edge over the other. Both countries increased their espionage efforts. Russia started sending what we call 'Sleeper Cells' to the United States, to enter our society and mix with the populous. Each one of the twenty people or so in the 'cells' had a specific target assignment. The agent was to seek out young people, particularly college students with backgrounds in science, computer operations, electrical systems, and mathematics, and become involved with them, to extract any information that could be utilized by Russia. You got caught in the middle, by association, since you and Chris were seeing each other on a regular basis. We really weren't sure what you knew."

"About four or five years ago, one of the agents, Svetlana Durisckoff, a.k.a. **Taylor Wagner**, was assigned to Chris Logan, who had a brother in the Navy SEAL Team unit. She was to get close to him and find out what he knew of his brother's assignments, what types of equipment he was using, where he was based, and so on. JD Logan was a Navy SEAL instructor and a communications and weapon specialist. The origin of the Seals began during World War II and Korea. Back then they were known as UDT (Underwater Demolition Teams). He was assigned to SEAL Team Two. JD became the 'Go to' person for clandestine operations. He had a little ritual that he went through right before he went 'down range' with his team. He wrote letters to his family, with instructions to mail the letters if he didn't return. When he did return safely, he would retrieve them and tear them up. He wanted everything to those who cared for him. He was pure Navy SEAL. His integrity and loyalty to his team are legendary from those early times. SEAL teams were just coming into their own, and the only thing anybody knew about their missions was 'It never happened. We were never there'. Keep in mind that she was to get close to Chris, even get romantically involved if necessary, to complete her mission."

"Taylor found out through College registries where Chris was going to school, and registered. She was about twenty-six, but could easily pass for twenty. She applied for the job in the cafeteria so she could 'accidently' meet Chris and develop a relationship with him. The Russian handlers had provided her with background data for her target and for herself. She went after Chris to obtain information on clandestine operations of the United States. Unfortunately for the Russians, Chris couldn't make up his mind about her and their 'love affair' fizzled, shutting down her part of the operation."

Elise closed her eyes and shuttered at the 'love affair' comment.

"When Taylor returned to New York she was re-assigned, and went 'under the radar', so to speak. She didn't surface again for a year, and, again it was trying to obtain information on our Special Operations groups. So much for the FIRST part of the story."

Elise broke in.

"Wait," She said, leaning forward on her chair, "Wait". Are you telling me Chris and I lost our future together because of an espionage operation neither of us knew anything about?"

"I'm afraid so, Mrs. Potter," Special Agent Winfield replied.

"Actually, it's better you didn't know anything about it. It keeps you above reproach."

"The SECOND phase of the operation was this: Chris wasn't able to return to college, and was unemployed. The draft was active then, and it looked like he was going to end up as a foot soldier if he didn't opt for another branch of service. With his skills, the Air Force convinced him to join their branch of service. He was unaware that the Russians had had him targeted and continued surveillance because of his skills in electronics and computers. Computer science was blossoming by leaps and bounds. When he joined the Air Force, a Russian mole in the Air Force Training Assignment Section managed to get Chris a Top Secret Crypto Q-4 clearance, so he could be assigned to a highly classified project known as 'The 4 Apostles'. He was sent for electronics, computer training, and specialty training at Keesler Air Force Base in Mississippi because of his computer skills. On top of that, the mole arranged for top secret orders to be given when he finished his electronics training to be transferred to a classified base out in Arizona. This is the base that handles all the testing on new equipment and clandestine operations material. What they hoped would happen was after he was trained and knew what the project was all about, he would disappear, with the Russians help, but not with his consent. We got wind of this, and after Chris's training, we foiled his kidnapping without him knowing a thing about the operation. To this day, Chris has no idea what role he played in this espionage case."

Elise just sat back and took it all in.

"Do you have any questions, Mrs. Potter?" Agent Winfield asked.

Elise thought for a moment.

"Will the Russians try to get to Chris again? Is he in any danger?"

Special Agent Winfield leaned forward in the chair.

"I rather doubt it, Mrs. Potter. You see, we've shut down the 'cell', and most of the group that was after Chris are either under indictment for espionage or have been deported. There's no more players in the game. Your husband will be managing Phase Two of the project. I suspect you'll get your clearance verified by early next week, and your husband will begin his job the following Monday."

Special Agent Winfield rose from the chair and headed for the door, Elise following him close behind.

"Thank you for putting my mind at ease, Agent Winfield," Elise said as she opened the door, and walked to the driveway with him.

"This has relieved my mind so much."

"Remember, not a word, and I was never here," Agent Winfield articulated as he slid onto the front seat of his car.

Elise simply nodded her head 'yes', folded her arms in front of her, and walked back to the house. She halfway laughed as she went, due to the irony of the situation and thought to herself, *'That's my Chris. He foils an espionage plan to obtain vital covert operations information, for a Russian agent, because he can't make up his mind about how he feels about her - and never knows it - then ends up training in a top-secret facility, and is saved from being kidnapped by the Department of Defense – and still doesn't know it. Had he BEEN kidnapped, he may have inadvertently started a nuclear war... and he was totally clueless. Yes, indeed, that's my Chris!*

Elise walked back into the house, and went upstairs to her bedroom. She walked over to her jewelry box, and opened the bottom tray, moving her hand to the back of the tray, grasping an object she put in the tray every night, removed it, and walked over to her rocker, and sat down holding the object close to her heart. It was a set of Air Force Instructor wings with a torch in the middle.

Elise rocked back and forth slowly, clutching the wings to her heart, thinking about Chris. She smiled as she remembered their times together.' If only, Chris...,' she sighed, 'If only...'

Chapter 20

Out of the past

Time moved forward. First a decade, then every year after that. During that time, Chris had gone to Craig/Sanderson College and received his Bachelor of Science in Biology degree and Medical Technology Certification. He now was a Medical Technologist in a major hospital laboratory and a paramedic, teaching Basic and Advanced Life Support in two universities and three technical schools. What was not known was that he was still on call for the Four Apostles project.

Through the years, his friend, Lance Brennen, had kept in touch with him. Lance had gone to medical school and had an orthopedic practice in Tucson, Arizona. They had discussed Elise many times while they were on duty at Keesler Air Force Base, and in letters they exchanged throughout the intervening years. Chris had told him that Elise had married and was now living near Tucson and was working somewhere in one of the hospitals as an OR nurse. He called one day to tell Chris that Elise had scrubbed in with him on a hip replacement case. He said she was a great OR nurse, and worked well with him. During conversation during the operation, Elise mentioned that she had two children, a boy, Jason, and a girl, Cassy. Her husband worked as a mechanical engineer and draftsman.

Lance never mentioned that he knew who she was or that they had been corpsman together in the Air Force. He wasn't sure if Chris wanted her to know that he was in contact with me. Chris told him to just leave things as they were. Chris had moved on, was married with a son, Joseph, who became a pilot for Delta Airlines and a daughter, Kimberly, who became a veterinarian, and a wife, Jesse, who was working for a large financial firm. Chris didn't want to upset things at this point in his life or in Elise's life.

Chris was kept busy in the hospital lab by day, and working with the paramedics on weeknights and weekends. He enjoyed the paramedics, because of all the additional training Chris had in the Air Force. Most of the time was spent on teaching or evaluating new medics.

Chris remembered a night he was working with one of the paramedic rescue units. The unit had been called to a house because a lady was having chest pain. He went in the house with the new medic, to evaluate his performance. The patient was a young woman about twenty- five years of age, sitting on an ottoman, breathing normally, but complained of chest pain in the lower anterior quadrant of the left lung. It appeared to be a mild anxiety attack, but they had to make sure.

The medic began his patient examination evaluation. Chris was standing behind the young lady, to her right side and was completing the evaluation record on the medic. Chris noticed that she had started giggling. Then, as he moved forward, around her right side, she said to the medic,' Do you want to put that thing in your ears?'

The medic had put his stethoscope around his neck to check for heart and lung sounds, and placed the flat chest piece on her chest and was moving it from point to point. The only trouble was that he positioned his hand on the end of the stethoscope in such a way that he was fondling her. He had completely forgotten to put the ear pieces in his ears! Then, when she saw that he wasn't REALLY listening to the chest sounds, she had to say something.

The medic was immediately replaced, and one of the other medics finished the hands-on evaluation. The medic received a three-day non-pay suspension, and a reprimand from the Hospital Medic Command Center.

Chris received a call at the lab a year or so later from Lance, one he wasn't prepared for.

"Sorry I had to track you down, Chris, but I thought you would want to know. You know that nurse you were involved with?"

Chris felt what was coming.

Lance got quiet, then told him what he feared most.

"Chris, I read in the paper this morning that Elise was killed in a traffic accident yesterday on the state highway. I'm sorry, Chris, I know how you felt about her. She left our service here and became chief scrub nurse at another hospital, so it's been a while since I've seen her. Is there anything I can do for you?"

Chris was numb from what Lance had just said. After about ten seconds, he answered him.

"Yeah, Lance, would you send flowers with a card, please? Don't say it's from me, just ask the florist to write on the card: "To a very special person who helped me understand what life's all about…with deepest sympathies to her family. From a fellow colleague,"

Chris thanked Lance, and then slowly returned the receiver to its cradle. Elise was gone forever. His life was now heading for its final chapter.

Chapter 21

The Reunion – Present Day

Cassy looked across the space between them, and hesitated to speak for a moment.

"What's wrong, Cassy?", Chris asked.

She looked straight at Chris, and folded her hands like her mother use to do.

"Chris, it's just that I got you over here under false pretenses. You said in your email that you wanted to know about Mom after she went through nurse's training, and what happened to her after that. You asked about her death."

"Chris, Mom didn't die in a car accident. It was another person with the same first name, and last name. Mom's signature was always 'Elise **L.** Potter... The other person's name was Elise Potter, no middle initial. Mom WAS in a car accident, but didn't die in the crash and has been alive all this time. I showed her the email from you, and asked her what she wanted me to do."

"Dad passed away eight years ago, and Mom returned home here to the Pittsburgh area. I own the house now. My grand-parents sold the house to me, and moved to Florida. I take care of Mom because of medical problems and injuries she received in the accident. She had no idea where you were, or how to contact you, but she wanted to see you. She asked me to contact you because of your ad in the paper requesting information about her. So, I sent a message to you at your email. And here you are. If you turn around, you'll see someone who has waited and wanted to see you for a long, long time. It's Mom, Chris..."

Cassy pointed toward the dining room.

Chris turned his head and looked in the direction of the dining room. Elise was standing there looking at Chris and smiling. She was wearing blue slacks, flats, a light blue angora sweater with a 'cow collar', On the left side of the sweater, she was wearing a set of Air Force Instructor's wings, the ones he had given to her before he left on his top-secret mission. All these years, she had kept them. Chris's lifetime unraveled before him. It felt as if he had just left her yesterday. He could hardly believe it! Elise was just looking at him, her head tilted slightly to one side, she spoke to Chris with her usual soft tone." Hi, Chris, miss me?"

Those words came rushing back to him from time gone passed. He stood there, not being able to move or speak. Tears formed in Chris's eyes.

"Elise," Chris began when he could finally speak, "You have no idea how many times during my life I was feeling down and lonely, my mind kept wandering back to you, and wouldn't let go. Our being together, frozen in time for me to keep within my heart."

Chris's mind was caught up in all the memories of her. Their first dance together at the 'Y', the Nurse's Ball (How much he wanted to tell her he loved her that night!), the times he spent in the evenings walking on the Biloxi, Mississippi beaches, thinking of her. The times he would go and sit on the beach, looking out over the water, and wonder what she was doing right then. He wrote a poem while visiting the beach one night:

Long Ago and Far Away

Long ago and far away,
Sunset's glory on the bay,
Things of past I now can see,
Gliding there in front of me.

Sunny days… your friendly smile,
Things that made my life worthwhile…
Rolling greens, and timbers tall…
Problems heard… Though great or small…

Times we talked, and times we cried…
Times we needed God to guide…
Times we spent in happiness…
Times our hearts were filled with bliss.

You were always close to me…
You… alone … would hear my plea…
You would make my darkness light…
Now, my Love… you're gone from sight…

Time goes on… as so must I…
Though in this world … alone … I cry…
And mem'ries of the past will stay…
… of long ago and far away!

Visiting her at Seaton Hill College, seeing her for the first time in her student nurse uniform. Even the day they separated. Memories of the past inundated him as he gazed on her face.

They walked slowly towards each other, their arms outstretched. Their eyes met and they moved in and out of each other's souls once more as they had done so long ago. Their hands touched, and they stood there as one, their bodies, minds, and souls melting together.

"I thought you had passed away in a car crash years ago. I didn't know."

"Elise, Angel, you have no idea how I felt, knowing that I would never see you again, never hold you again, never tell you how much a part of my life you are, never being able to hold you and tell you, I love you."

"There were so many times throughout my life I wished that you were with me, sharing an experience. I finally realized what you were trying to say in that letter you sent to me after we separated.... The part where you told me about the young doctor on an episode of that medical series drama, when he read the letter from the love of his life...'...**It is dark ... I am in my room... I am alone... and I am crying ... because you are so far away... and because I love you so very much...**' I've *lived* those words for over fifty years..."

"I should never have left you. You were the turning point in my life, and I chose to walk away from the one I really loved and who loved me, to another life of immediate satisfactions and a lifetime of searching for what was ALREADY mine."

Their embrace was now in that moment in time when their emotions ran the gamut of what they felt for each other.

"I never want to be without you again, Elise."

Chris ran his hand slowly and deliberately over her face and through her tresses, which now were white, taking in her beauty and remembering those quiet moments together that faded into visions of times shared.

Elise pulled away slightly and gazed into Chris's eyes, laying her hand on his chest.

"There's a secret I've kept all my life." Her voice trembled as their eyes met. "I never stopped loving you, even after we stopped seeing each other. There were nights I cried myself to sleep. Sometimes I would be somewhere that we had been or I would remember something we had shared together. The feelings I first felt for you would come rushing back. I never gave up hope that we would be together, someday."

"I wore your wings, pinned to my nurse's uniform, every work day of my life. Even being married, I couldn't let go. I always took them off before I went home. I didn't want to hurt Bill."

Cassy had quietly excused herself. Elise and Chris stood there in the living room, not letting the other go. How much time went by before they sat down on the couch together, Chris didn't know. Chris never wanted to let go of her again.

"I'm glad I heard what you told Cassy," Elise said quietly to Chris, their hands squeezing together, then moving up and down each other's arms.

"I'm guessing you still love me," Elise whispered to Chris.

Chapter 22

Feelings Revisited

Elise and Chris talked about their lives that spanned fifty years. Their marriages, their children, their careers, their times alone, all the things that life brings to us. Chris told Elise his wife, Jesse, had passed away from lymphocytic leukemia three years prior. Chris had retired shortly after that and he now owned a small home on ten acres outside of Washington, Pennsylvania. The children had grown and long since left their childhood home. He was filling in for a medical tech school instructor not far from his home twice a week teaching laboratory procedures. It kept his mind active. He didn't mention he was still on call for top-secret government projects.

As always, time passed swiftly when they were together, and once more, it was time for Chris to leave. They had held on to each other not wanting to let go, and their hearts searched the lifetime within them, and their once young love blossomed again in their hearts.

Chris gradually stood up, moving back slightly.

"When will I see you again?", Chris asked.

Elise rose slowly, placed her hands on either side of his face.

They kissed,

"Is tomorrow to soon, my Love?" she answered.

Her answer made Chris's old life fade away and his new life begin. Chris's life was in the light of all he had dreamed of since their eyes first met, and their worlds swirled together in a universe of horizons yet to be seen. They were one once more as their souls entwined.

Chris put his coat on, and once more, their hands joined.

"I'll call you as soon as I get home. I love you, Elise. There are no more tomorrows without you."

They looked deeply into each other's eyes. Their eyes spoke those silent thoughts you can't put into words, but their hearts knew their thoughts and filled their very beings with joy.

They walked to the door, and shared one last passionate kiss. Chris held her close, feeling the warmth of her body next to his, not wanting this time with her to end.

"Bring my dream back to me, Chris. I love you," Elise whispered to him as they stepped away from their embrace.

Chris opened the door, stepped out onto the porch, walked down the steps to his car and waved to Elise as he backed down the driveway and drove up the road.

The trip home was the longest hour and a half Chris had ever experienced. His thoughts were racing, and his heart was filled with feelings he had felt in times gone by. Those feelings were from the past, and the present, mixed together in such a perfect way.

Chapter 23

Last Thoughts

As Chris drove up his driveway, he was anticipating talking to Elise again, seeing her, holding her, sharing their souls as their eyes told a love story to each other that no one could ever hear. Chris longed to tell her all the things he should have said decades ago.

Chris entered the house and went to his study to call her. He noticed a 'You've got Mail!' on the computer monitor as he sat at his desk. Chris opened the email, and saw it was from Cassy." Please call me as soon as you get this message … C."

Chris picked up the phone and dialed Cassy's number. It rang twice, and Cassy answered.

"Chris, I…..I don't know how to tell you this (her voice was trembling) …Mom,…… Mom passed away. After you left, Mom went to the living room window and watched as you drove down the road. When your car disappeared around the bend, she walked over to her chair, and sat down and stared out the window. She never seemed as happy as she was this afternoon. She pulled her legs up under her and tilted her head to the one side. I noticed she was smiling. A tear had run down her cheek. I went into the kitchen to start dinner, and twenty minutes later, I called to her to ask what she wanted to drink. She didn't answer, so I went into the living room."

"Mom, did you hear me?"

A moment before Cassy entered the room, Elise had closed her eyes, her heart rate was dropping, and her breathing was becoming shallow. She felt very tired. She smiled, even though her life was drifting away. Her mind wandered as she thought about seeing Chris's face, feeling his arms around her, his breath upon her cheek, his gentle caring touch, and the love they had both kept within their hearts throughout the years.

'Chris came back,... That's my Chris,...' she thought to herself. A few more seconds, and she said quietly her last words..." Chris ... I... love... you..."

And then she was gone.

She was just sitting there, with that same smile on her face. A tiny trace of a tear had left its path on the side of her cheek, and had faded onto her chin.

"She passed the way she wanted too, Chris. You made her life happy and complete. You really loved her. You came back."

Chris didn't know what to say.

"Is there anything I can do for you, Cassy?" Tears were filling Chris's eyes now, and his voice was cracking.

"No, Chris. I have final arrangements to make. I'll call you when they're complete."

"Thank you for letting me know," he managed to say, and hung the phone up.

His voice was low pitched, and his face was washed in tears.

He slumped back in the chair, exhausted, and closed his eyes to rest and reflect on his life past, especially the events that had occurred this day. Chris's quest over fifty years for his soulmate had left him alone and wanting, his heart empty. Chris had failed.

Chris must have fallen asleep, for how long, he didn't know. As he awoke, he opened his eyes hearing someone calling his name. The voice floated through the open study window on a gentle breeze, and surrounded him.

"Chris .... Chris ... You haven't failed .... You came back ... You came back to me ... Please, Darling... Come to me now...I'm waiting for you."

He couldn't believe what he was hearing! He knew the voice. It was Elise!

Chris turned and looked out of the window towards the field across the road. The pasture grass in the field moved back and forth in rhythm with the wind and the clover bowed gently. The evening autumn sky was alive with hues of color, as if painted by a master. The water in the brook moved slowly down its worn path on its way to the pasture's boundary. The huge oak tree on a small rise in the pasture released its leaves as the wind directed it. There, beneath the huge branches of the mighty oak, stood Elise. For the very first time, Chris could truly call her 'My Elise'.

Chris thought about the song he had once heard sung by Josh Groban: 'To Where You Are'. The last four line's words filled his mind.

'If only for a while to know you're there, **A breath away** not far to where you are. I know you're there. **A breath away not far to where you are.**'[1]

Before Chris realized what was happening, he was out of the house, down and across the road, and walking in the meadow toward the old oak. As he approached the edge of the brook, Chris could hear the soothing relaxing sounds of the water lapping against the banks of the brook.

He crossed the brook and walked up the small rise toward the oak tree where his Love was standing. She was young again. Her skin had the smooth alabaster softness she had in her youth. She was wearing a white chiffon dress like the one she wore to the Nurse's Ball. Her hair had returned to auburn from white, and was in a twist. The fading sunlight caused rays of glimmer to stream from her head as she turned towards Chris. A small, single diamond was suspended

---

1 Written by Richard Marks, by Linda Thompson and Alan Menken

from a gold chain around her neck, sparkling, as the light from the flaming sunset reflected off the facets of the diamond. Her hands were folded in front of her, and as their eyes met, it was the same look they had known the night they first looked towards each other setting their souls free to join with one another.

Somehow, Chris felt stronger, younger. His skin was no longer wrinkled, and his muscles moved with sincere determination as he walked. Chris wasn't tired anymore, and no longer needed his glasses. Chris's whole being became new before his eyes.

He looked at his hands. They were young and smooth again. His face was without wrinkles. His body no longer felt the pain of old age. Chris walked as tall and strong as he had at his high school graduation. They were both young again.

They walked towards each other, their eyes never losing contact. Chris thought he was in a dream, yet he knew he wasn't. It was the fulfillment of his hopes and dreams from all the years he was without her in his life.

They met each other half-way up the rise.

'*You are so beautiful*', Chris thought as he approached his Forever Love.

They raised their arms slowly, and placed their hands together, feeling warmth they had waited so long for.

"Miss me, Chris?" Elise asked as they embraced each other.

With that single statement, Chris knew he would never hear her ask that again. This time they were together, forever.

Chris didn't know what was happening, and he didn't care. He was engulfed in an intimate moment he chose to savor. What they were together was what they had held in the recesses of their hearts. They had an eternity to grow together, to love together, and to be together.

They shared a kiss that could have lasted as long as the stars shone. As their lips separated, their eyes could see what cannot be described here, for its beauty rested within their souls.

"Chris, I never want this to end." Elise said smiling.

Chris pulled her close to him.

"Neither do I, Angel, neither do I."

Their arms around each other, their eyes opened to what was ahead, their dreams lifting them up, their hearts filled with love, they ascended toward their destiny. Their love had begun with a simple look in each other's direction at a dance, and now was continuing into eternity. It took over fifty years to find what Chris had given up long ago, but he had not failed. He came back. They were now One, forever.

This, then, is truly the BEGINNING of their story……

www.ingramcontent.com/pod-product-compliance
Lightning Source LLC
Chambersburg PA
CBHW070450170726
48291CB00005B/1688

* 9 7 8 1 9 4 9 7 4 6 9 3 8 *